My Little Pony

Adventures in Friendship

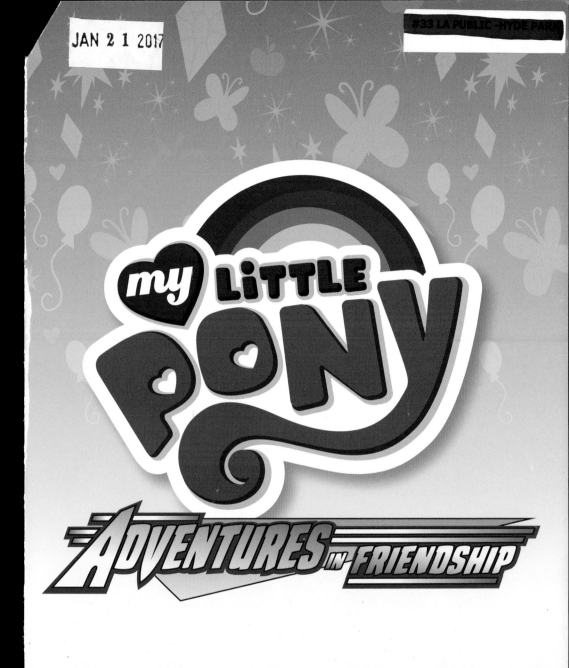

COVER BY SARA RICHARD
ORIGINAL SERIES EDITS BY BOBBY CURNOW
COLLECTION EDITS BY JUSTIN EISINGER AND ALONZO SIMON
COLLECTION DESIGN BY THOM ZAHLER
PUBLISHER TED ADAMS

Special thanks to Meghan McCarthy, Eliza Hart, Ed Lane, Beth Artale, and Michael Kelly.

ISBN: 978-1-63140-610-2   19 18 17 16   1 2 3 4

® Licensed By: Hasbro

www.IDWPUBLISHING.com

Ted Adams, CEO & Publisher
Greg Goldstein, President & COO
Robbie Robbins, EVP/Sr. Graphic Artist
Chris Ryall, Chief Creative Officer/Editor-in-Chief
Matthew Ruzicka, CPA, Chief Financial Officer
Dirk Wood, VP of Marketing
Lorelei Bunjes, VP of Digital Services
Jeff Webber, VP of Digital Publishing & Business Development
Jerry Bennington, VP of New Product Development

Facebook: facebook.com/idwpublishing
Twitter: @idwpublishing
YouTube: youtube.com/idwpublishing
Tumblr: tumblr.idwpublishing.com
Instagram: instagram.com/idwpublishing

Originally published as MY LITTLE PONY MICRO-SERIES #1: TWILIGHT SPARKLE and MY LITTLE PONY: FRIENDS FOREVER #4 and 26.

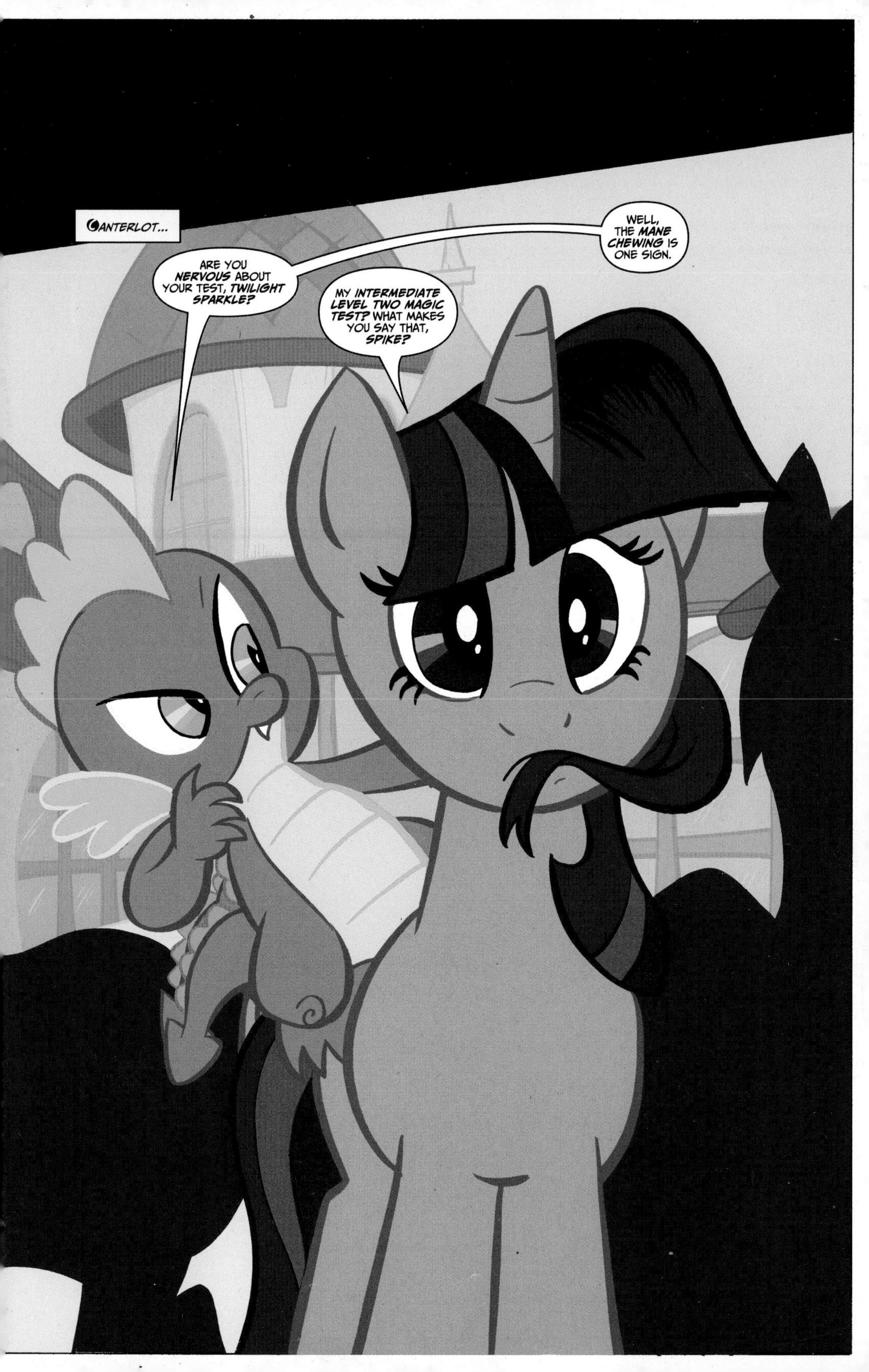
CANTERLOT...
ARE YOU NERVOUS ABOUT YOUR TEST, TWILIGHT SPARKLE?
MY INTERMEDIATE LEVEL TWO MAGIC TEST? WHAT MAKES YOU SAY THAT, SPIKE?
WELL, THE MANE CHEWING IS ONE SIGN.

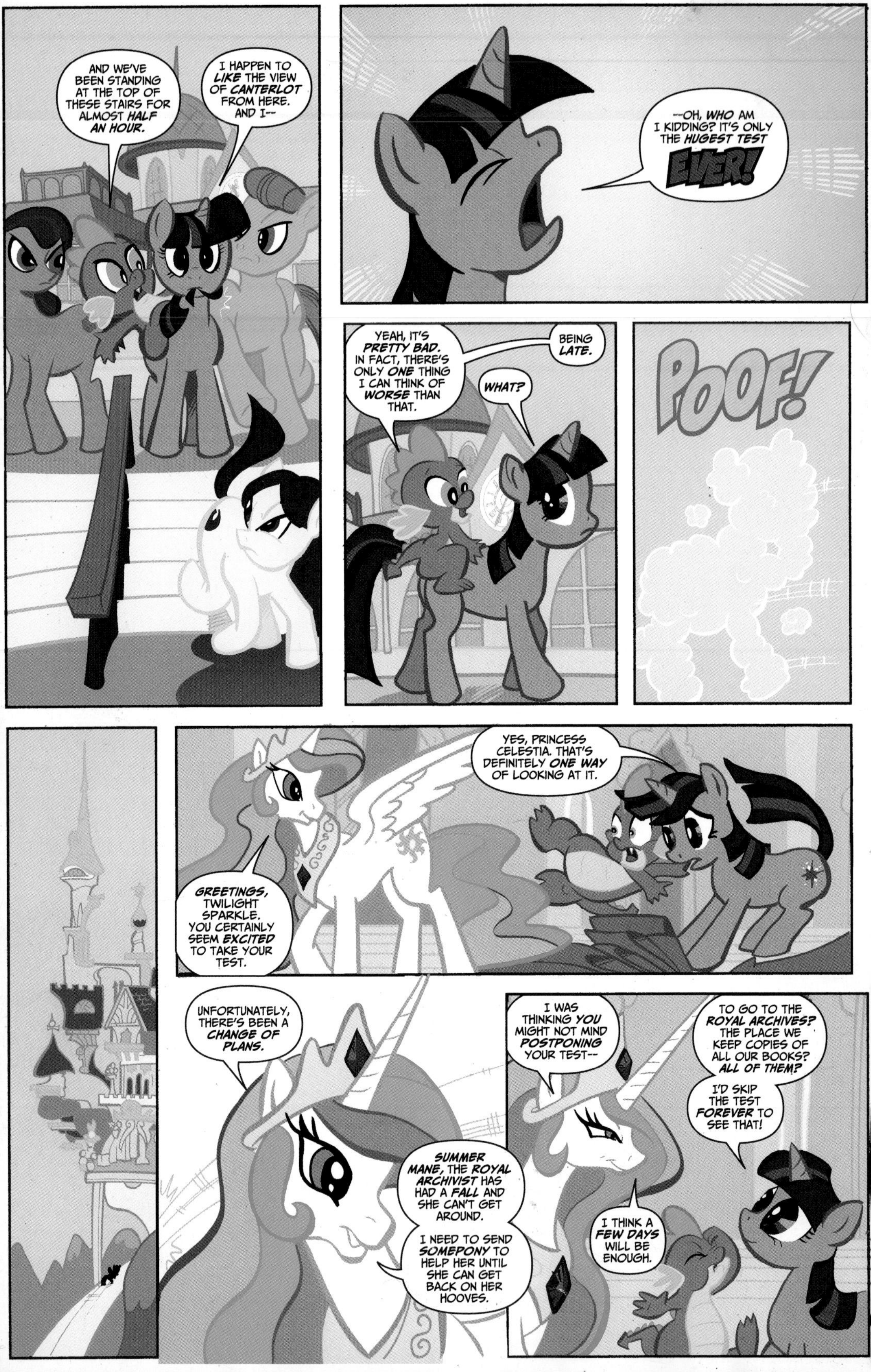
AND WE'VE BEEN STANDING AT THE TOP OF THESE STAIRS FOR ALMOST HALF AN HOUR.
I HAPPEN TO LIKE THE VIEW OF CANTERLOT FROM HERE. AND I--
--OH, WHO AM I KIDDING? IT'S ONLY THE HUGEST TEST EVER!
YEAH, IT'S PRETTY BAD. IN FACT, THERE'S ONLY ONE THING I CAN THINK OF WORSE THAN THAT.
WHAT?
BEING LATE.
POOF!
GREETINGS, TWILIGHT SPARKLE. YOU CERTAINLY SEEM EXCITED TO TAKE YOUR TEST.
YES, PRINCESS CELESTIA. THAT'S DEFINITELY ONE WAY OF LOOKING AT IT.
UNFORTUNATELY, THERE'S BEEN A CHANGE OF PLANS.
SUMMER MANE, THE ROYAL ARCHIVIST HAS HAD A FALL AND SHE CAN'T GET AROUND.
I NEED TO SEND SOMEPONY TO HELP HER UNTIL SHE CAN GET BACK ON HER HOOVES.
I WAS THINKING YOU MIGHT NOT MIND POSTPONING YOUR TEST--
TO GO TO THE ROYAL ARCHIVES? THE PLACE WE KEEP COPIES OF ALL OUR BOOKS? ALL OF THEM?
I'D SKIP THE TEST FOREVER TO SEE THAT!
I THINK A FEW DAYS WILL BE ENOUGH.

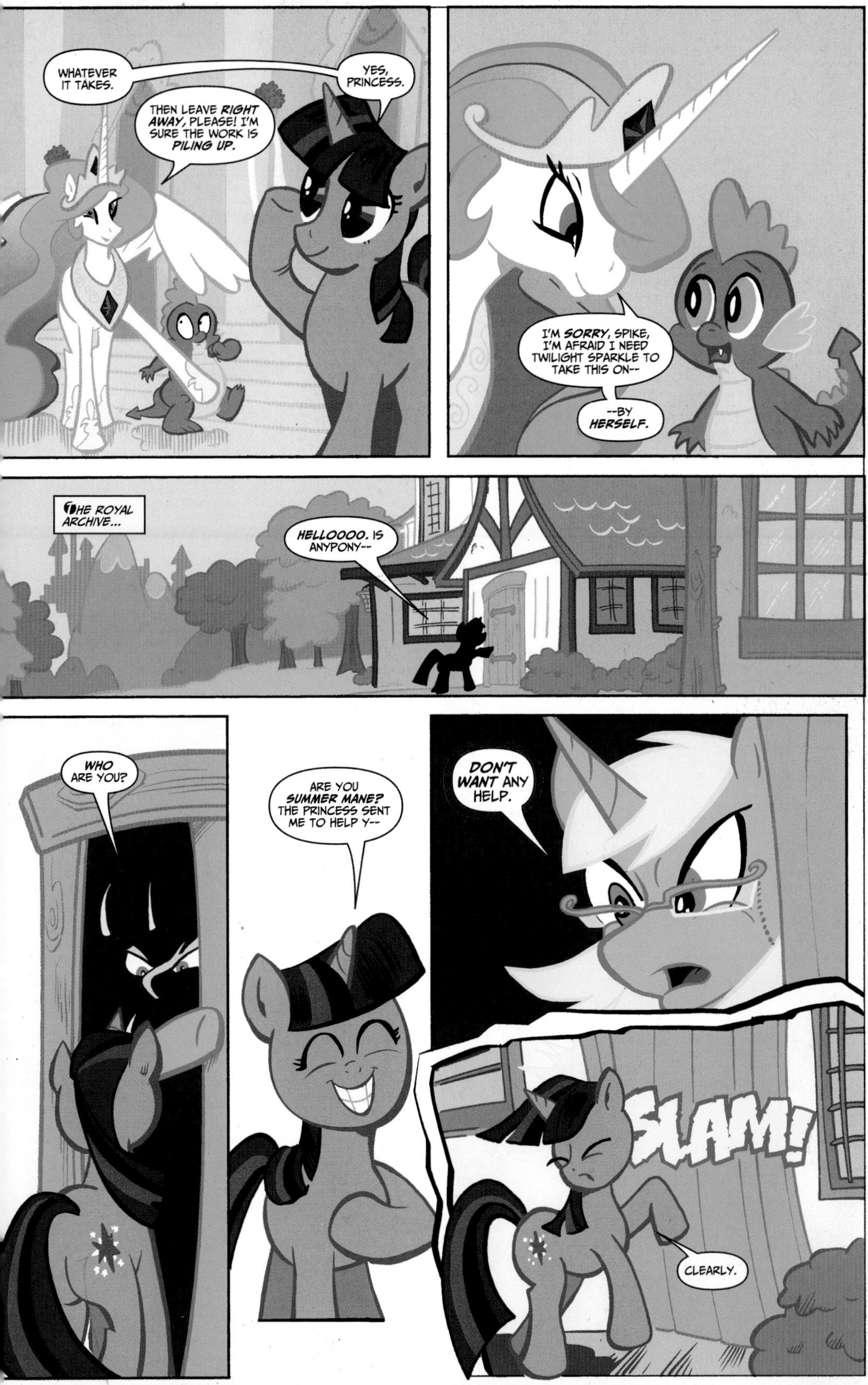

WHATEVER IT TAKES.
YES, PRINCESS.
THEN LEAVE RIGHT AWAY, PLEASE! I'M SURE THE WORK IS PILING UP.
I'M SORRY, SPIKE, I'M AFRAID I NEED TWILIGHT SPARKLE TO TAKE THIS ON--
--BY HERSELF.
THE ROYAL ARCHIVE...
HELLOOOO. IS ANYPONY--
WHO ARE YOU?
ARE YOU SUMMER MANE? THE PRINCESS SENT ME TO HELP Y--
DON'T WANT ANY HELP.
SLAM!
CLEARLY.

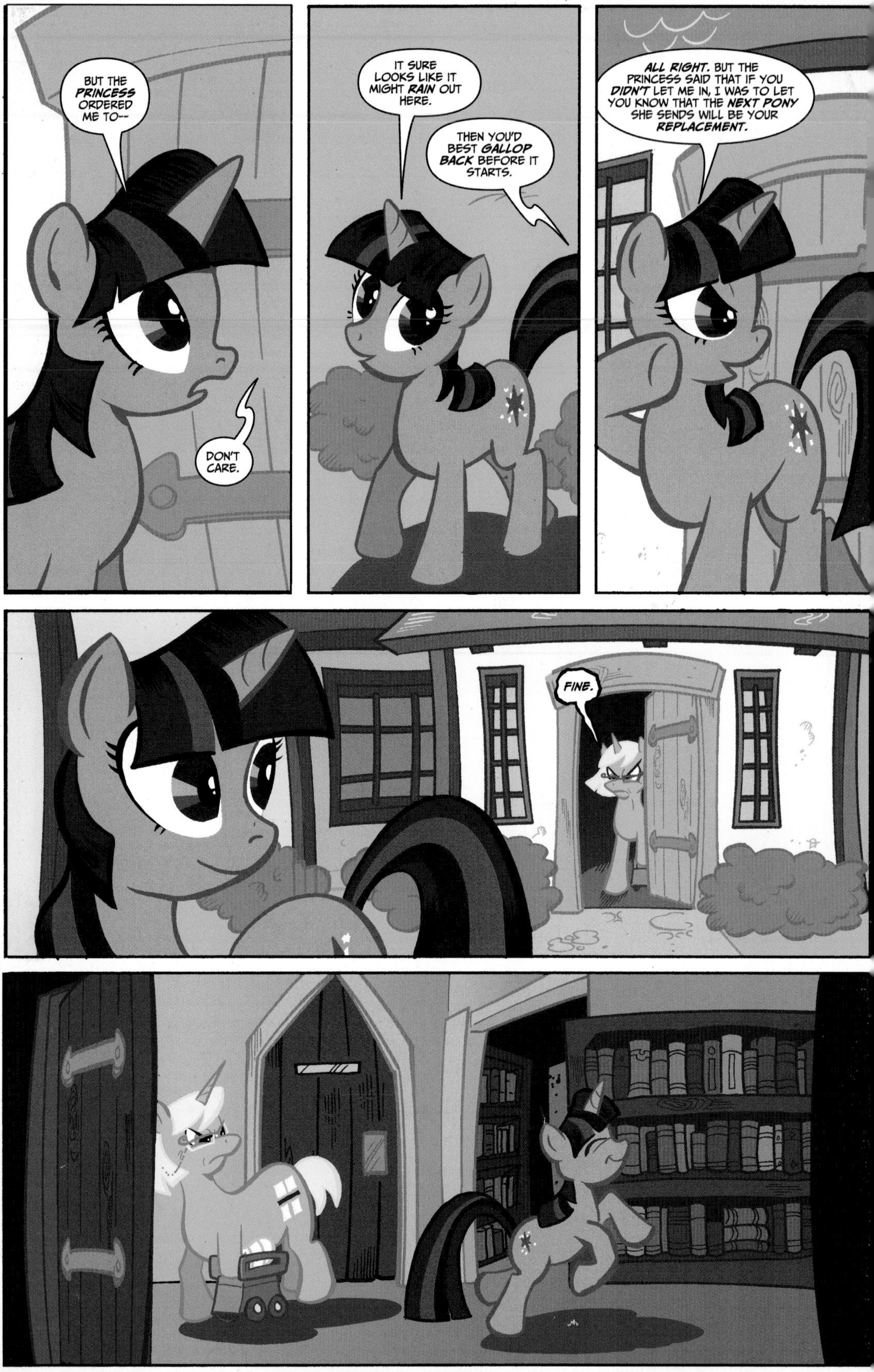

BUT THE PRINCESS ORDERED ME TO--
DON'T CARE.
IT SURE LOOKS LIKE IT MIGHT RAIN OUT HERE.
THEN YOU'D BEST GALLOP BACK BEFORE IT STARTS.
ALL RIGHT. BUT THE PRINCESS SAID THAT IF YOU DIDN'T LET ME IN, I WAS TO LET YOU KNOW THAT THE NEXT PONY SHE SENDS WILL BE YOUR REPLACEMENT.
FINE.

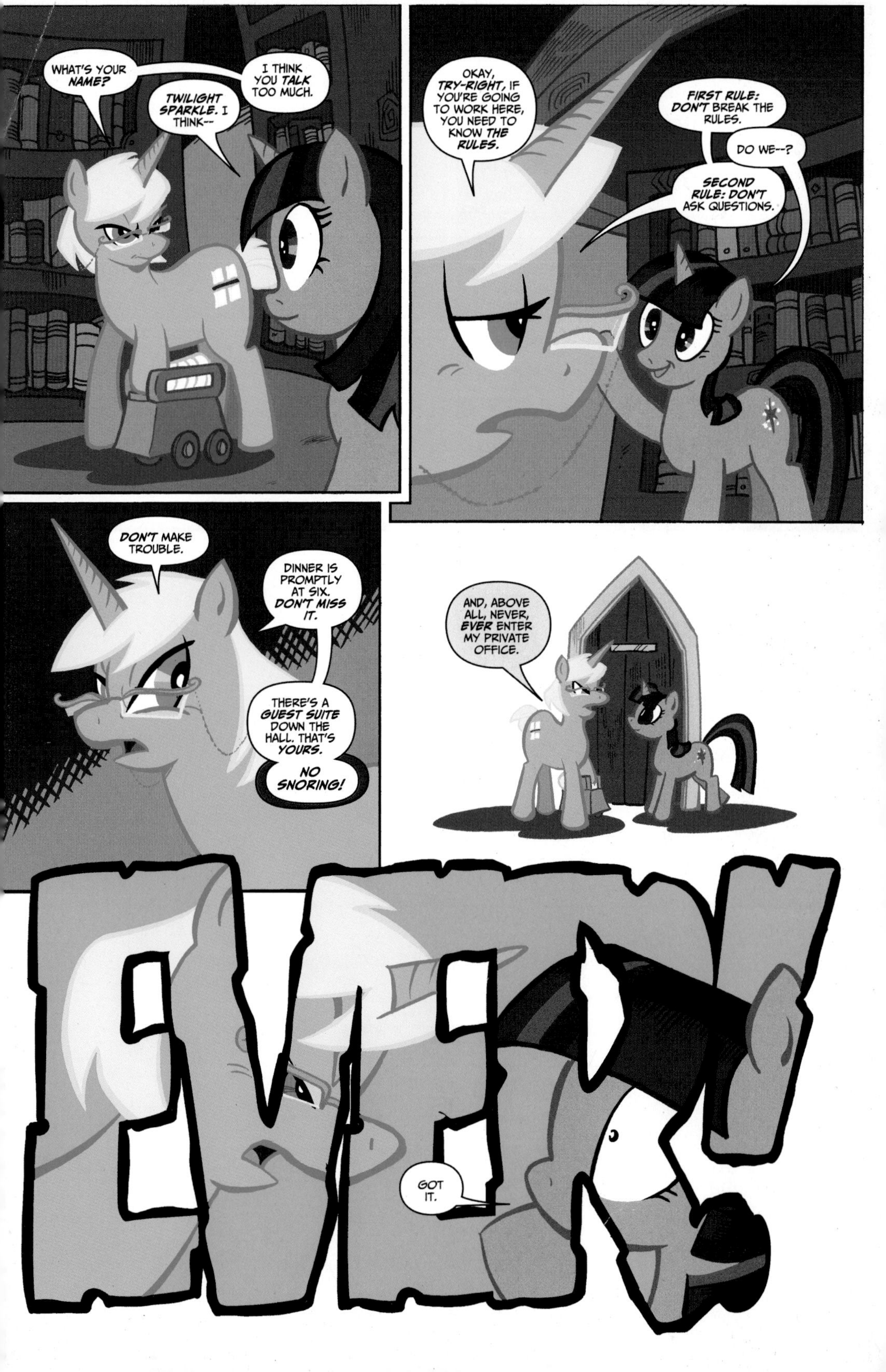

WHAT'S YOUR NAME?
TWILIGHT SPARKLE. I THINK--
I THINK YOU TALK TOO MUCH.
OKAY, TRY-RIGHT, IF YOU'RE GOING TO WORK HERE, YOU NEED TO KNOW THE RULES.
FIRST RULE: DON'T BREAK THE RULES.
DO WE--?
SECOND RULE: DON'T ASK QUESTIONS.
DON'T MAKE TROUBLE.
DINNER IS PROMPTLY AT SIX. DON'T MISS IT.
THERE'S A GUEST SUITE DOWN THE HALL. THAT'S YOURS.
NO SNORING!
AND, ABOVE ALL, NEVER, EVER ENTER MY PRIVATE OFFICE.
EVER!
GOT IT.

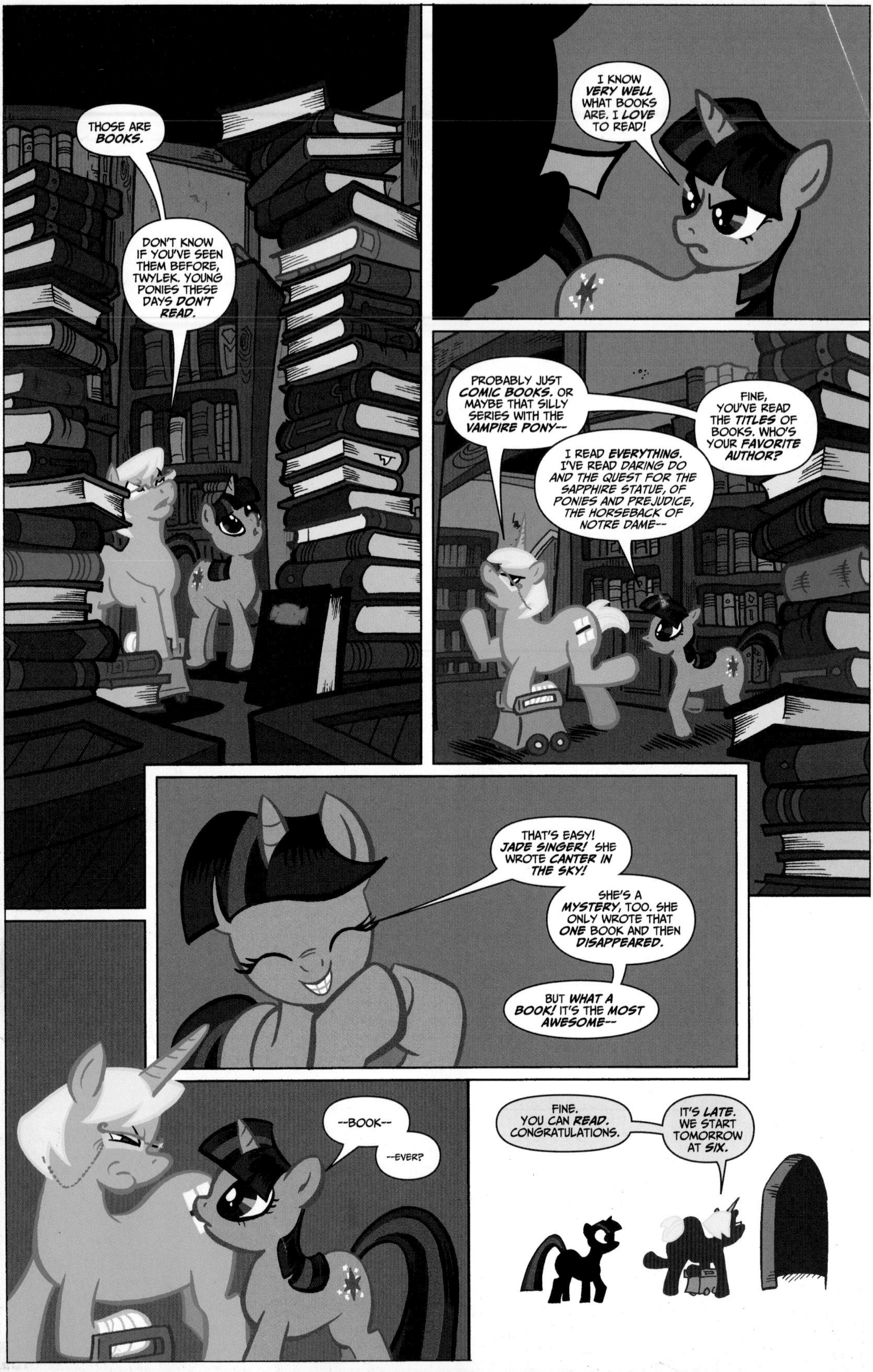
THOSE ARE BOOKS.
DON'T KNOW IF YOU'VE SEEN THEM BEFORE, TWYLEK. YOUNG PONIES THESE DAYS DON'T READ.
I KNOW VERY WELL WHAT BOOKS ARE. I LOVE TO READ!
PROBABLY JUST COMIC BOOKS. OR MAYBE THAT SILLY SERIES WITH THE VAMPIRE PONY--
I READ EVERYTHING. I'VE READ DARING DO AND THE QUEST FOR THE SAPPHIRE STATUE, OF PONIES AND PREJUDICE, THE HORSEBACK OF NOTRE DAME--
FINE, YOU'VE READ THE TITLES OF BOOKS. WHO'S YOUR FAVORITE AUTHOR?
THAT'S EASY! JADE SINGER! SHE WROTE CANTER IN THE SKY!
SHE'S A MYSTERY, TOO. SHE ONLY WROTE THAT ONE BOOK AND THEN DISAPPEARED.
BUT WHAT A BOOK! IT'S THE MOST AWESOME--
--BOOK--
--EVER?
FINE. YOU CAN READ. CONGRATULATIONS.
IT'S LATE. WE START TOMORROW AT SIX.

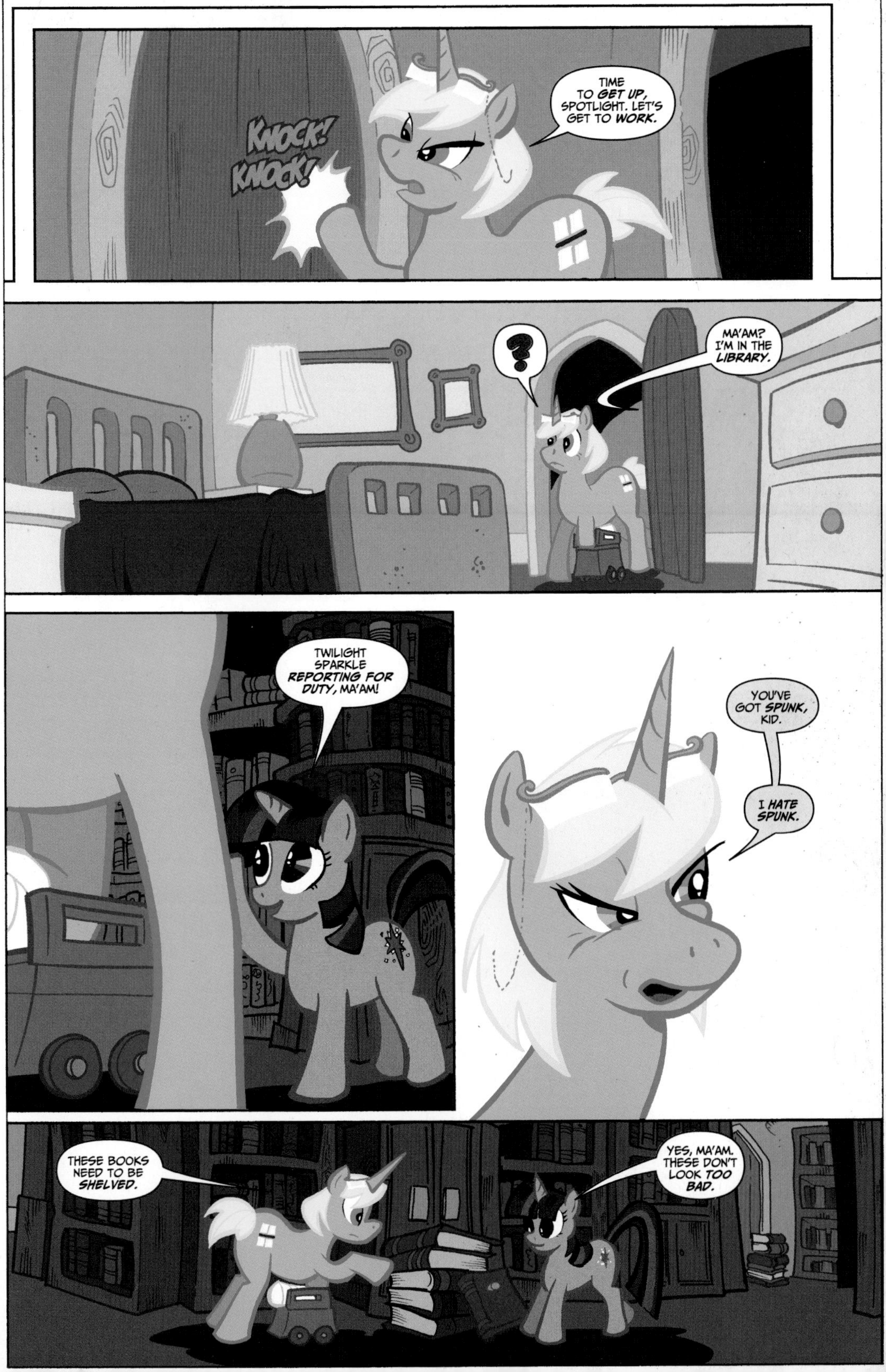
KNOCK! KNOCK!
TIME TO GET UP, SPOTLIGHT. LET'S GET TO WORK.
?
MA'AM? I'M IN THE LIBRARY.
TWILIGHT SPARKLE REPORTING FOR DUTY, MA'AM!
YOU'VE GOT SPUNK, KID.
I HATE SPUNK.
THESE BOOKS NEED TO BE SHELVED.
YES, MA'AM. THESE DON'T LOOK TOO BAD.

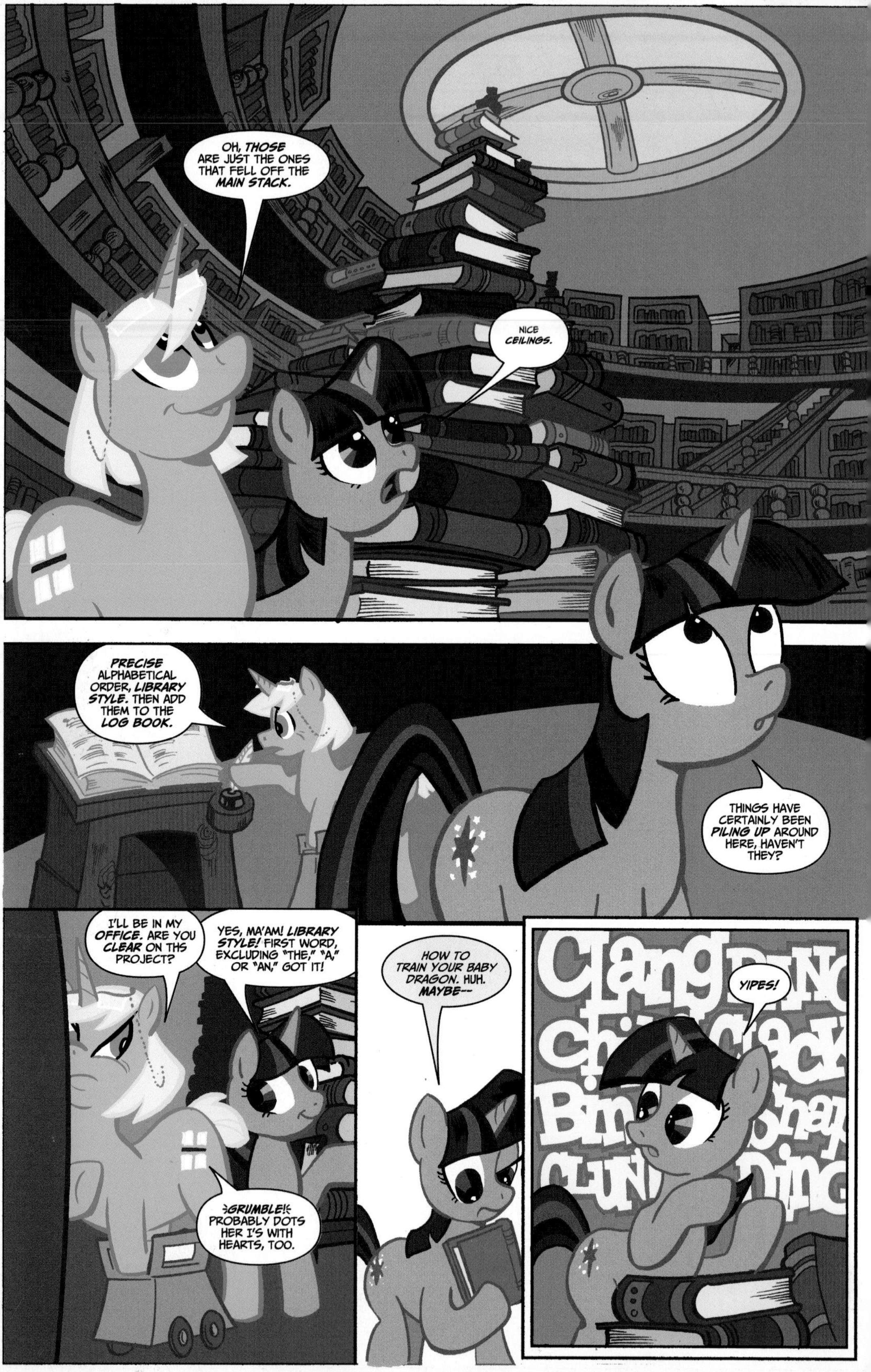
OH, THOSE ARE JUST THE ONES THAT FELL OFF THE MAIN STACK.
NICE CEILINGS.
PRECISE ALPHABETICAL ORDER, LIBRARY STYLE. THEN ADD THEM TO THE LOG BOOK.
THINGS HAVE CERTAINLY BEEN PILING UP AROUND HERE, HAVEN'T THEY?
I'LL BE IN MY OFFICE. ARE YOU CLEAR ON THS PROJECT?
YES, MA'AM! LIBRARY STYLE! FIRST WORD, EXCLUDING "THE," "A," OR "AN," GOT IT!
GRUMBLE! PROBABLY DOTS HER I'S WITH HEARTS, TOO.
HOW TO TRAIN YOUR BABY DRAGON. HUH. MAYBE--
YIPES!

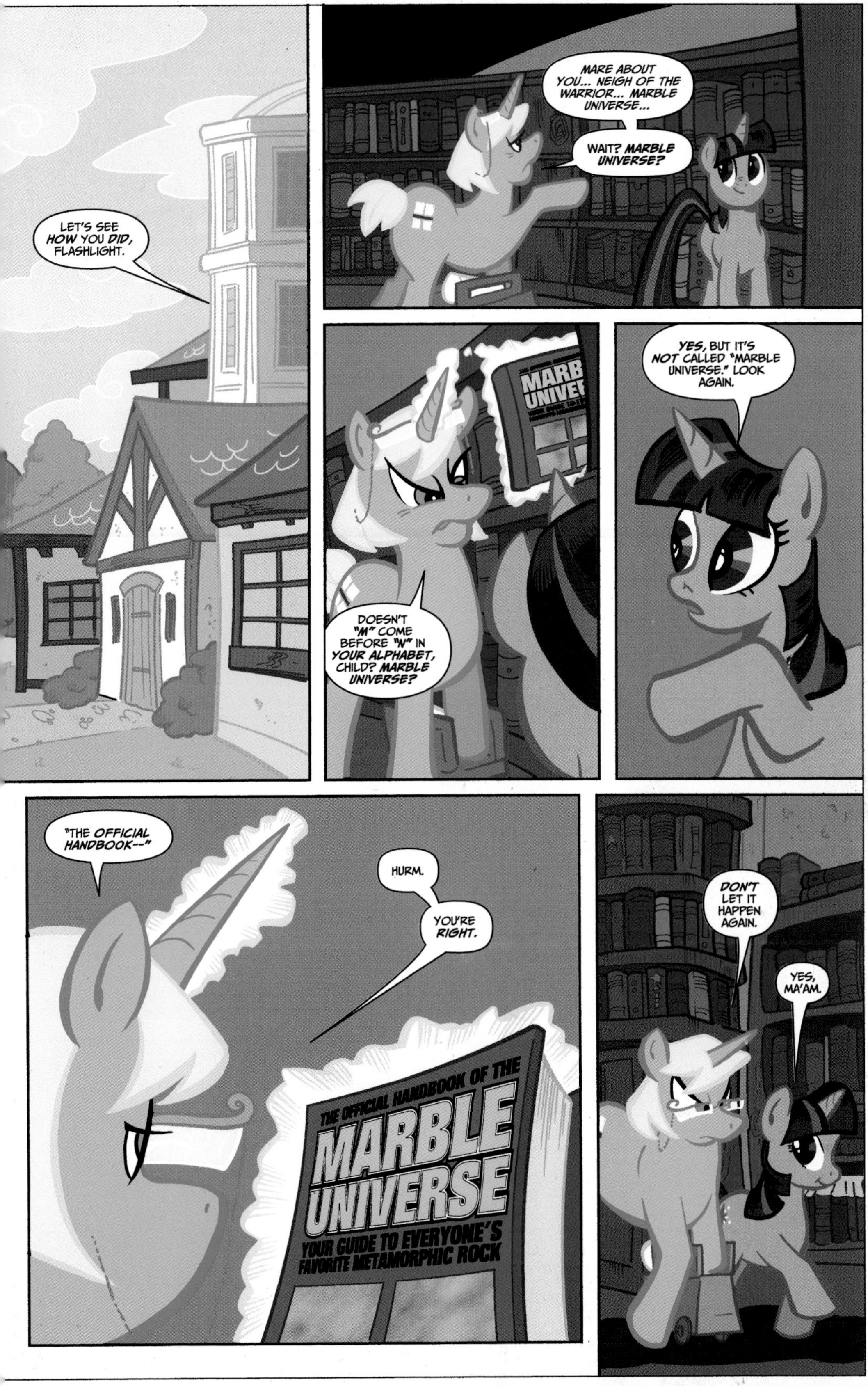
LET'S SEE HOW YOU DID, FLASHLIGHT.
MARE ABOUT YOU... NEIGH OF THE WARRIOR... MARBLE UNIVERSE...
WAIT? MARBLE UNIVERSE?
DOESN'T "M" COME BEFORE "W" IN YOUR ALPHABET, CHILD? MARBLE UNIVERSE?
YES, BUT IT'S NOT CALLED "MARBLE UNIVERSE." LOOK AGAIN.
"THE OFFICIAL HANDBOOK--"
HURM.
YOU'RE RIGHT.
THE OFFICIAL HANDBOOK OF THE
MARBLE UNIVERSE
YOUR GUIDE TO EVERYONE'S FAVORITE METAMORPHIC ROCK
DON'T LET IT HAPPEN AGAIN.
YES, MA'AM.

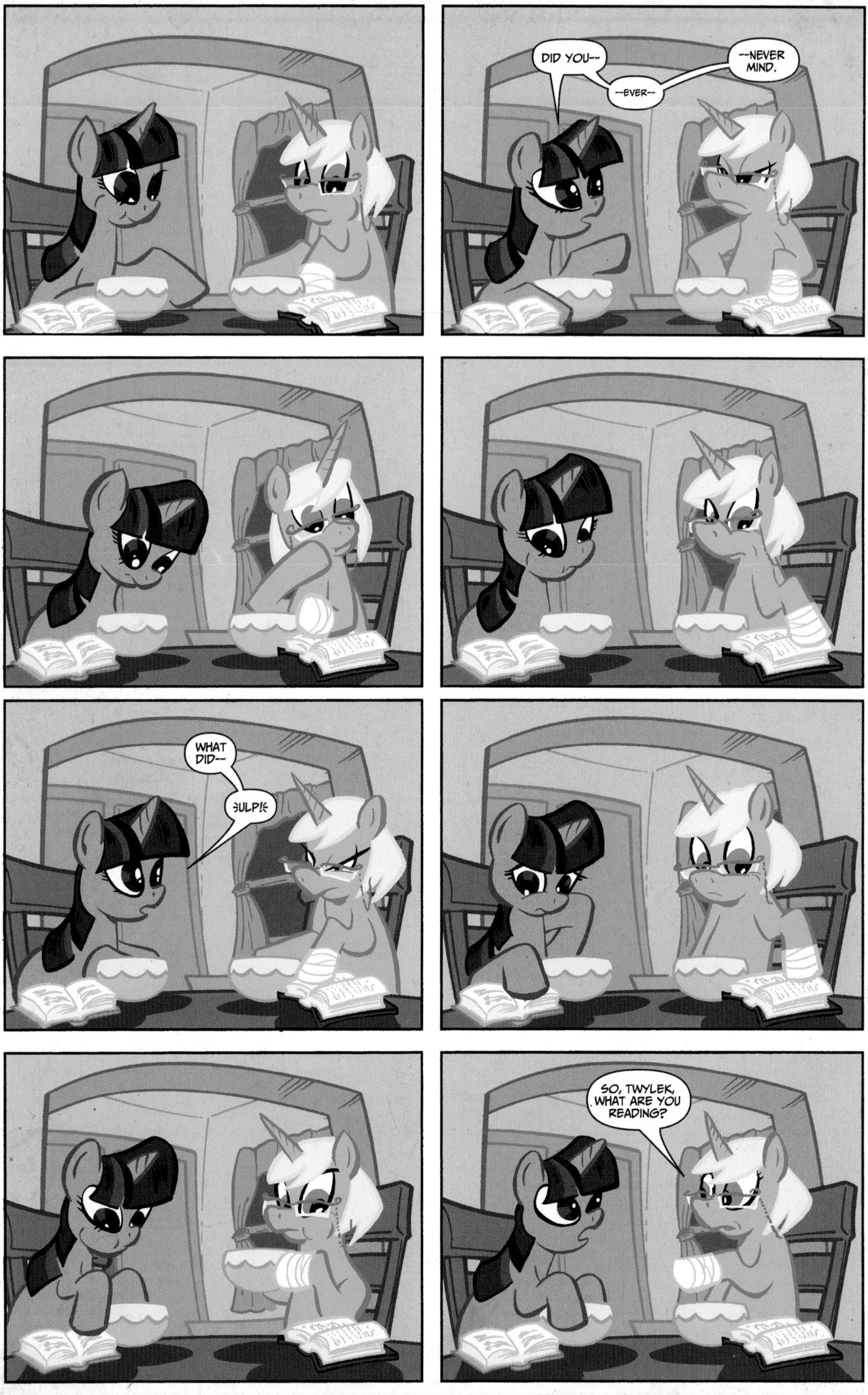
DID YOU--
--EVER--
--NEVER MIND.
WHAT DID--
ULP!
SO, TWYLEK, WHAT ARE YOU READING?

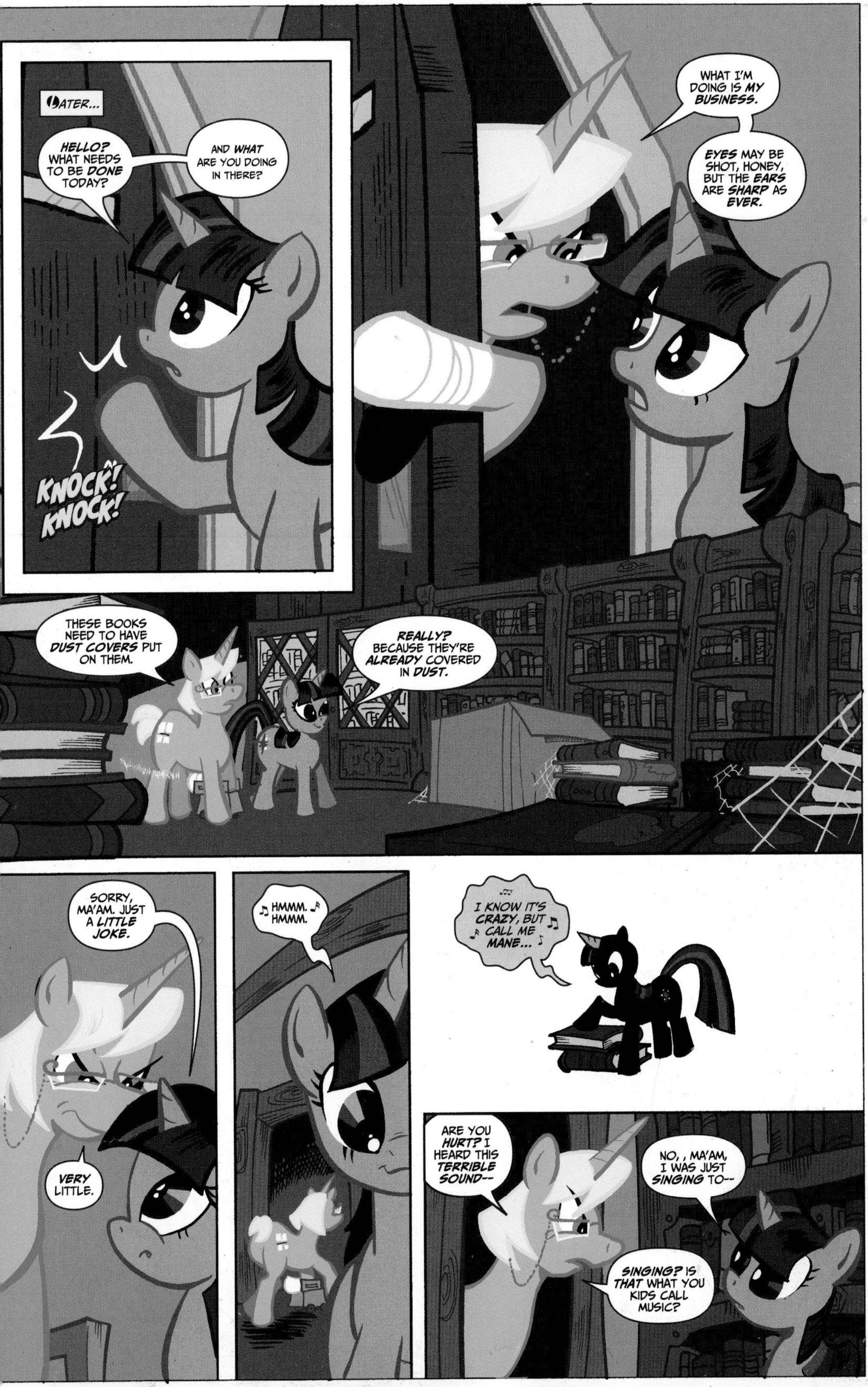

LATER...
HELLO? WHAT NEEDS TO BE DONE TODAY?
AND WHAT ARE YOU DOING IN THERE?
KNOCK! KNOCK!
WHAT I'M DOING IS MY BUSINESS.
EYES MAY BE SHOT, HONEY, BUT THE EARS ARE SHARP AS EVER.
THESE BOOKS NEED TO HAVE DUST COVERS PUT ON THEM.
REALLY? BECAUSE THEY'RE ALREADY COVERED IN DUST.
SORRY, MA'AM. JUST A LITTLE JOKE.
VERY LITTLE.
HMMM. HMMM.
I KNOW IT'S CRAZY, BUT CALL ME MANE...
ARE YOU HURT? I HEARD THIS TERRIBLE SOUND--
NO, , MA'AM, I WAS JUST SINGING TO--
SINGING? IS THAT WHAT YOU KIDS CALL MUSIC?

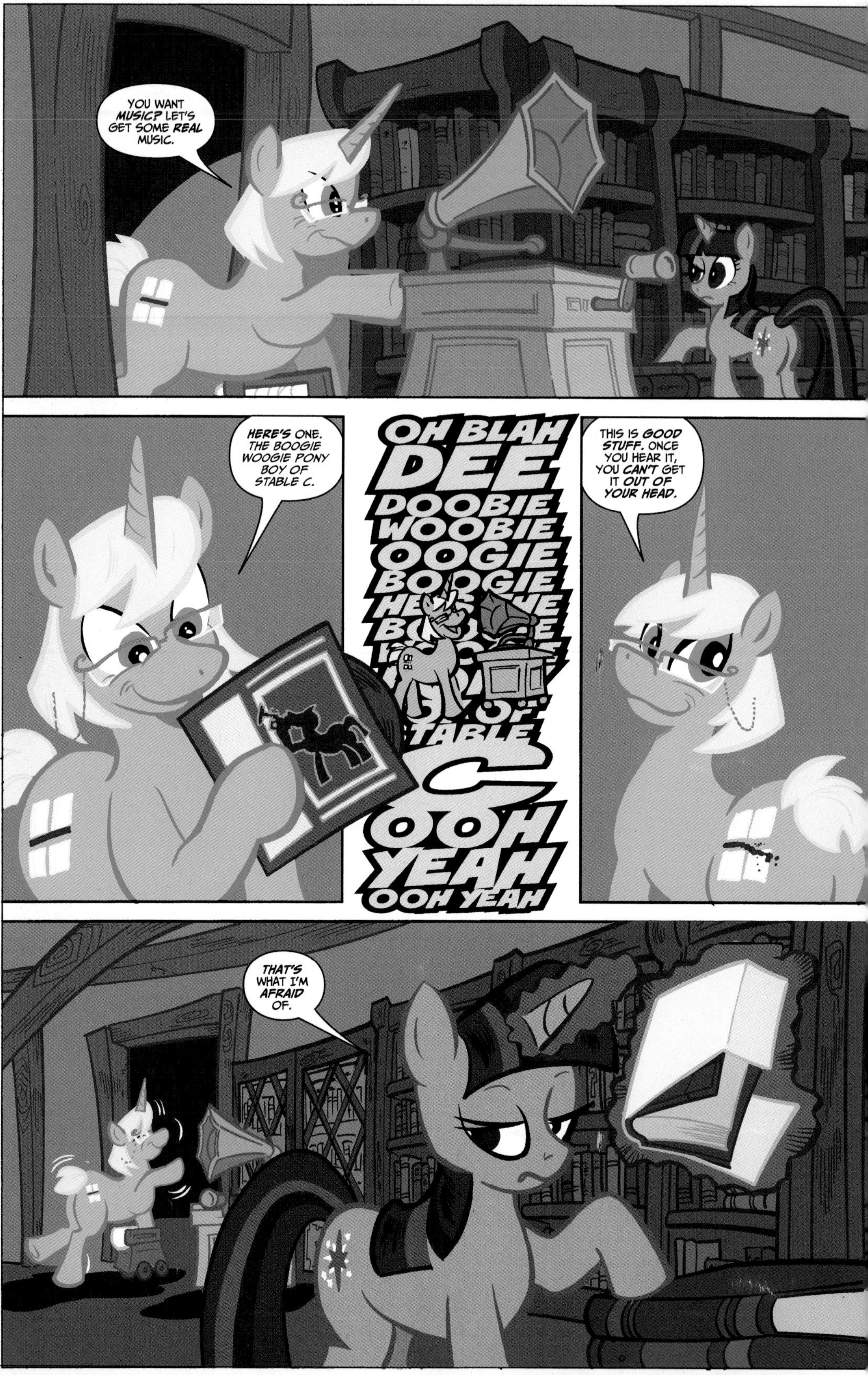
YOU WANT MUSIC? LET'S GET SOME REAL MUSIC.
HERE'S ONE. THE BOOGIE WOOGIE PONY BOY OF STABLE C.
OH BLAH DEE DOOBIE WOOBIE OOGIE BOOGIE
STABLE C OOH YEAH OOH YEAH
THIS IS GOOD STUFF. ONCE YOU HEAR IT, YOU CAN'T GET IT OUT OF YOUR HEAD.
THAT'S WHAT I'M AFRAID OF.

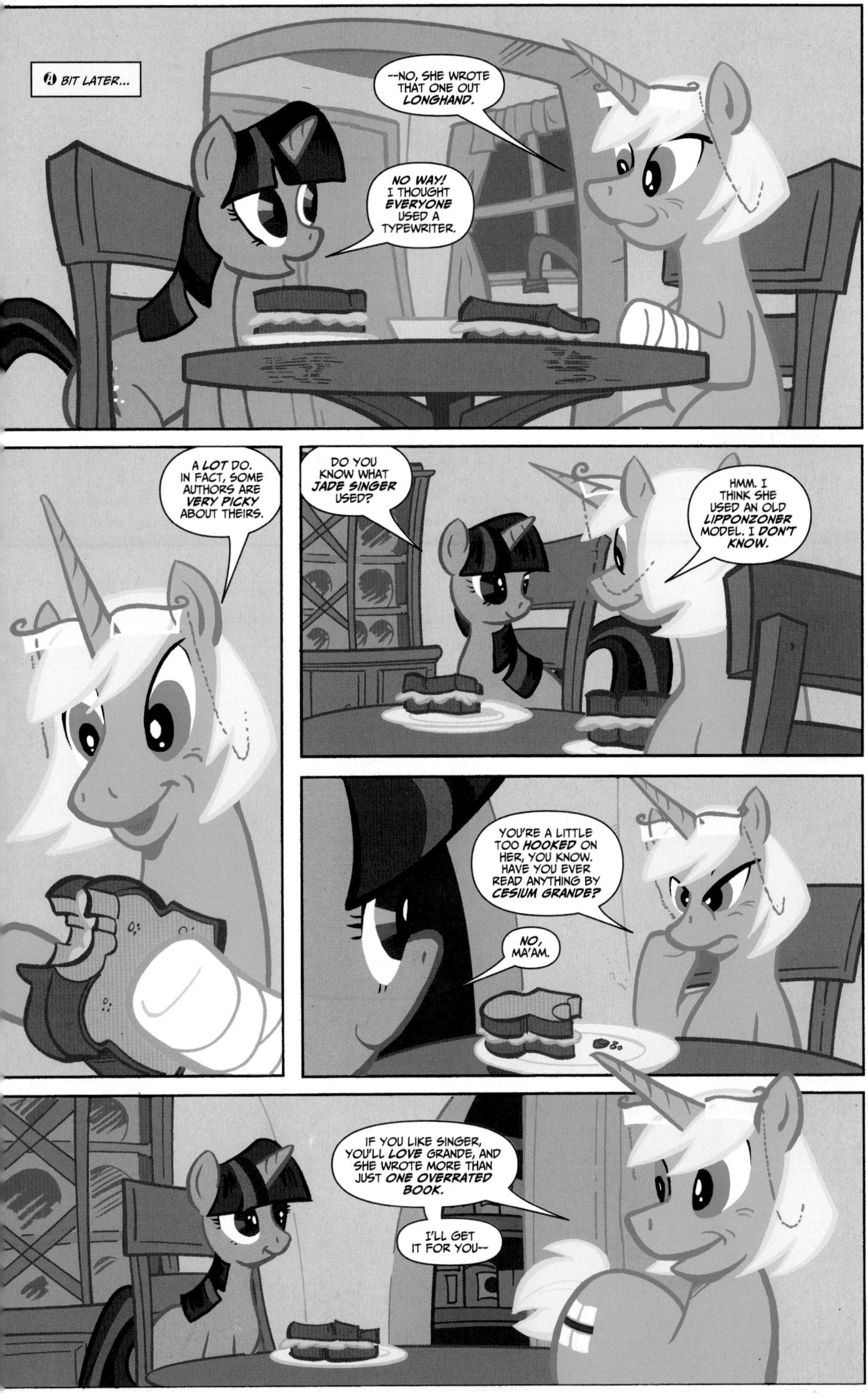
A BIT LATER...
--NO, SHE WROTE THAT ONE OUT LONGHAND.
NO WAY! I THOUGHT EVERYONE USED A TYPEWRITER.
A LOT DO. IN FACT, SOME AUTHORS ARE VERY PICKY ABOUT THEIRS.
DO YOU KNOW WHAT JADE SINGER USED?
HMM. I THINK SHE USED AN OLD LIPPONZONER MODEL. I DON'T KNOW.
YOU'RE A LITTLE TOO HOOKED ON HER, YOU KNOW. HAVE YOU EVER READ ANYTHING BY CESIUM GRANDE?
NO, MA'AM.
IF YOU LIKE SINGER, YOU'LL LOVE GRANDE, AND SHE WROTE MORE THAN JUST ONE OVERRATED BOOK.
I'LL GET IT FOR YOU--

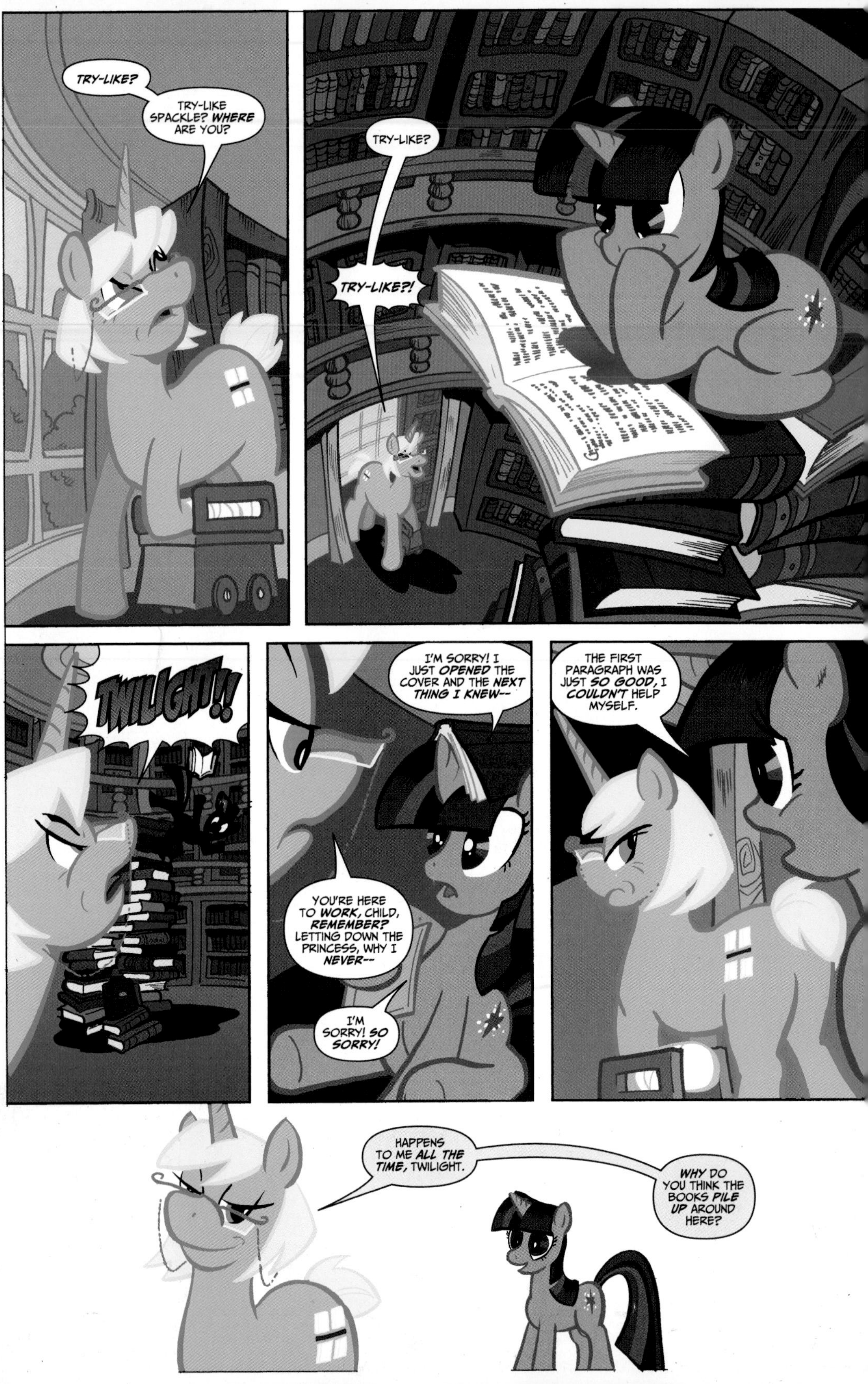
TRY-LIKE?
TRY-LIKE SPACKLE? WHERE ARE YOU?
TRY-LIKE?
TRY-LIKE?!
TWILIGHT!!
I'M SORRY! I JUST OPENED THE COVER AND THE NEXT THING I KNEW--
YOU'RE HERE TO WORK, CHILD, REMEMBER? LETTING DOWN THE PRINCESS, WHY I NEVER--
I'M SORRY! SO SORRY!
THE FIRST PARAGRAPH WAS JUST SO GOOD, I COULDN'T HELP MYSELF.
HAPPENS TO ME ALL THE TIME, TWILIGHT.
WHY DO YOU THINK THE BOOKS PILE UP AROUND HERE?

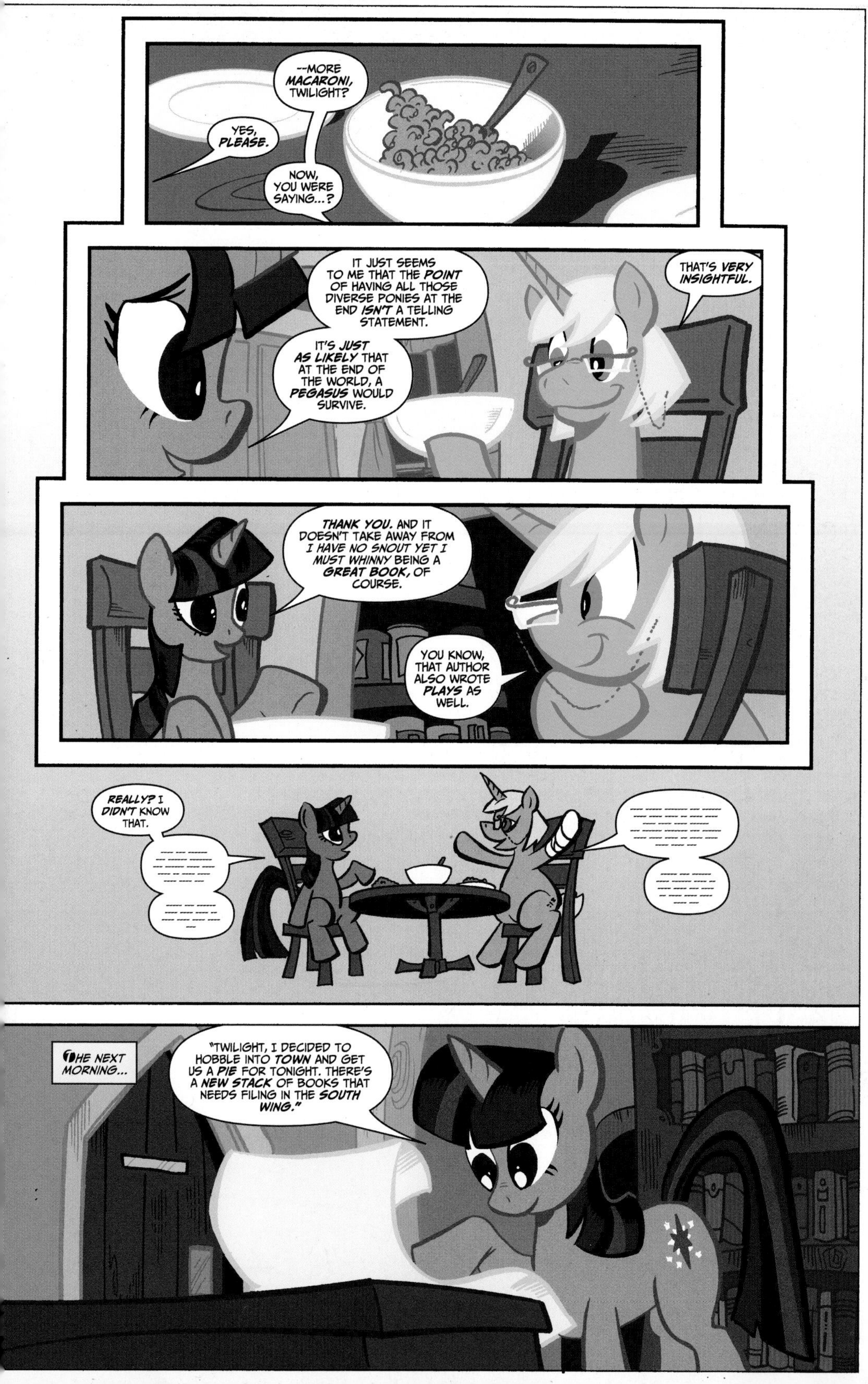
--MORE MACARONI, TWILIGHT?
YES, PLEASE.
NOW, YOU WERE SAYING...?
IT JUST SEEMS TO ME THAT THE POINT OF HAVING ALL THOSE DIVERSE PONIES AT THE END ISN'T A TELLING STATEMENT.
IT'S JUST AS LIKELY THAT AT THE END OF THE WORLD, A PEGASUS WOULD SURVIVE.
THAT'S VERY INSIGHTFUL.
THANK YOU. AND IT DOESN'T TAKE AWAY FROM I HAVE NO SNOUT YET I MUST WHINNY BEING A GREAT BOOK, OF COURSE.
YOU KNOW, THAT AUTHOR ALSO WROTE PLAYS AS WELL.
REALLY? I DIDN'T KNOW THAT.
THE NEXT MORNING...
"TWILIGHT, I DECIDED TO HOBBLE INTO TOWN AND GET US A PIE FOR TONIGHT. THERE'S A NEW STACK OF BOOKS THAT NEEDS FILING IN THE SOUTH WING."

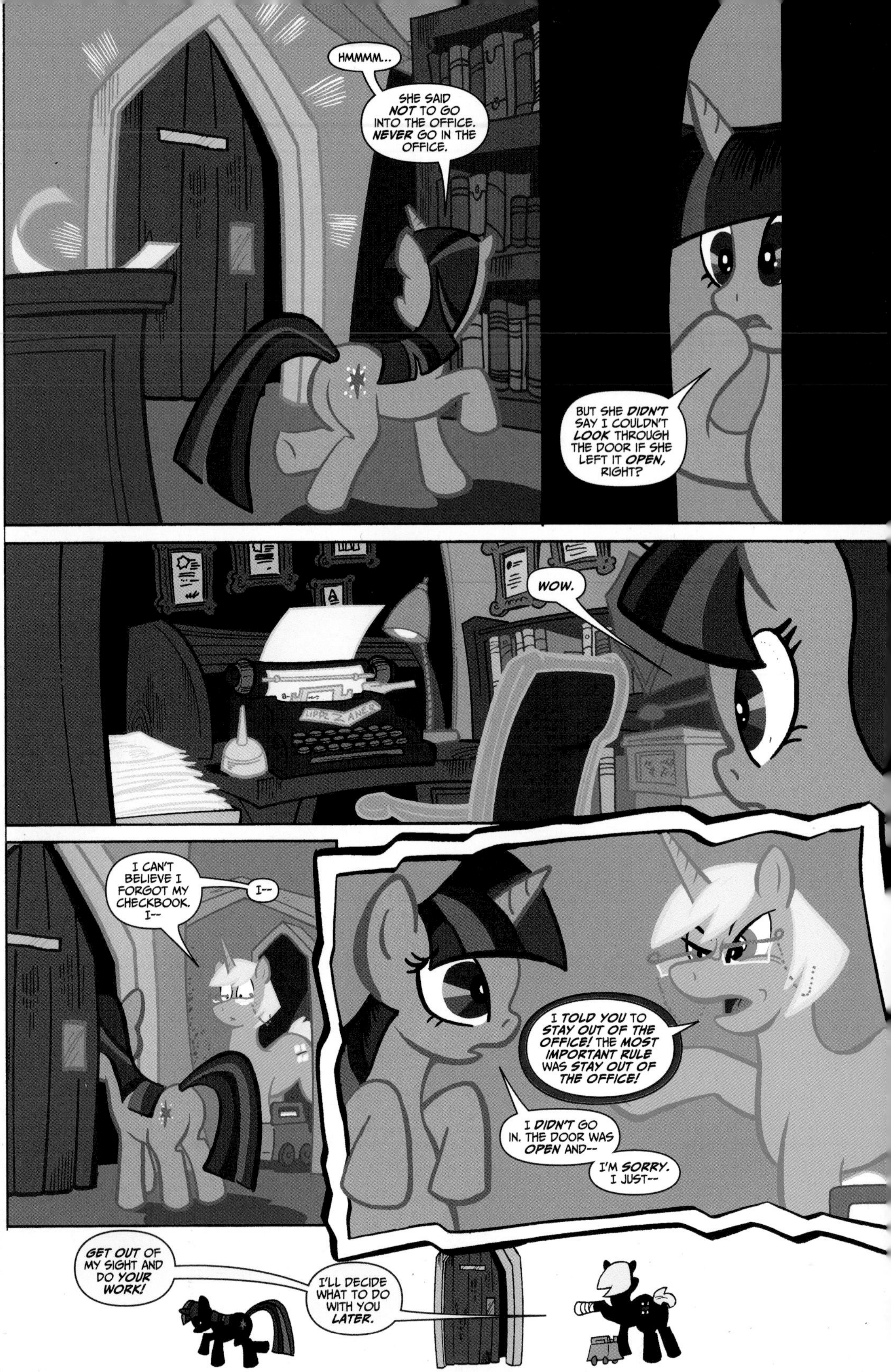

HMMMM...
SHE SAID NOT TO GO INTO THE OFFICE. NEVER GO IN THE OFFICE.
BUT SHE DIDN'T SAY I COULDN'T LOOK THROUGH THE DOOR IF SHE LEFT IT OPEN, RIGHT?
LIPPIZANER
WOW.
I CAN'T BELIEVE I FORGOT MY CHECKBOOK. I--
I--
I TOLD YOU TO STAY OUT OF THE OFFICE! THE MOST IMPORTANT RULE WAS STAY OUT OF THE OFFICE!
I DIDN'T GO IN. THE DOOR WAS OPEN AND--
I'M SORRY. I JUST--
GET OUT OF MY SIGHT AND DO YOUR WORK!
I'LL DECIDE WHAT TO DO WITH YOU LATER.

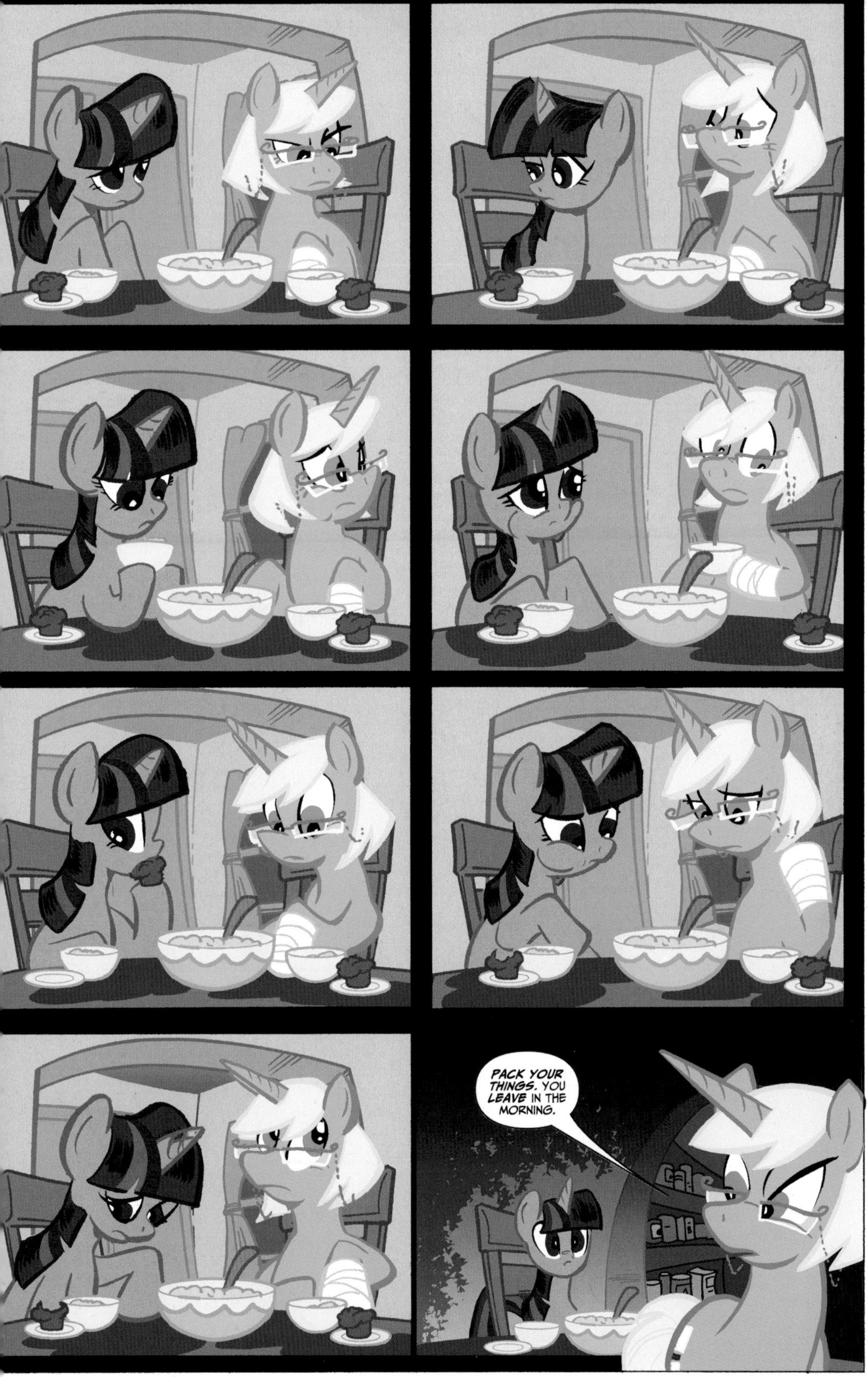
PACK YOUR THINGS. YOU LEAVE IN THE MORNING.

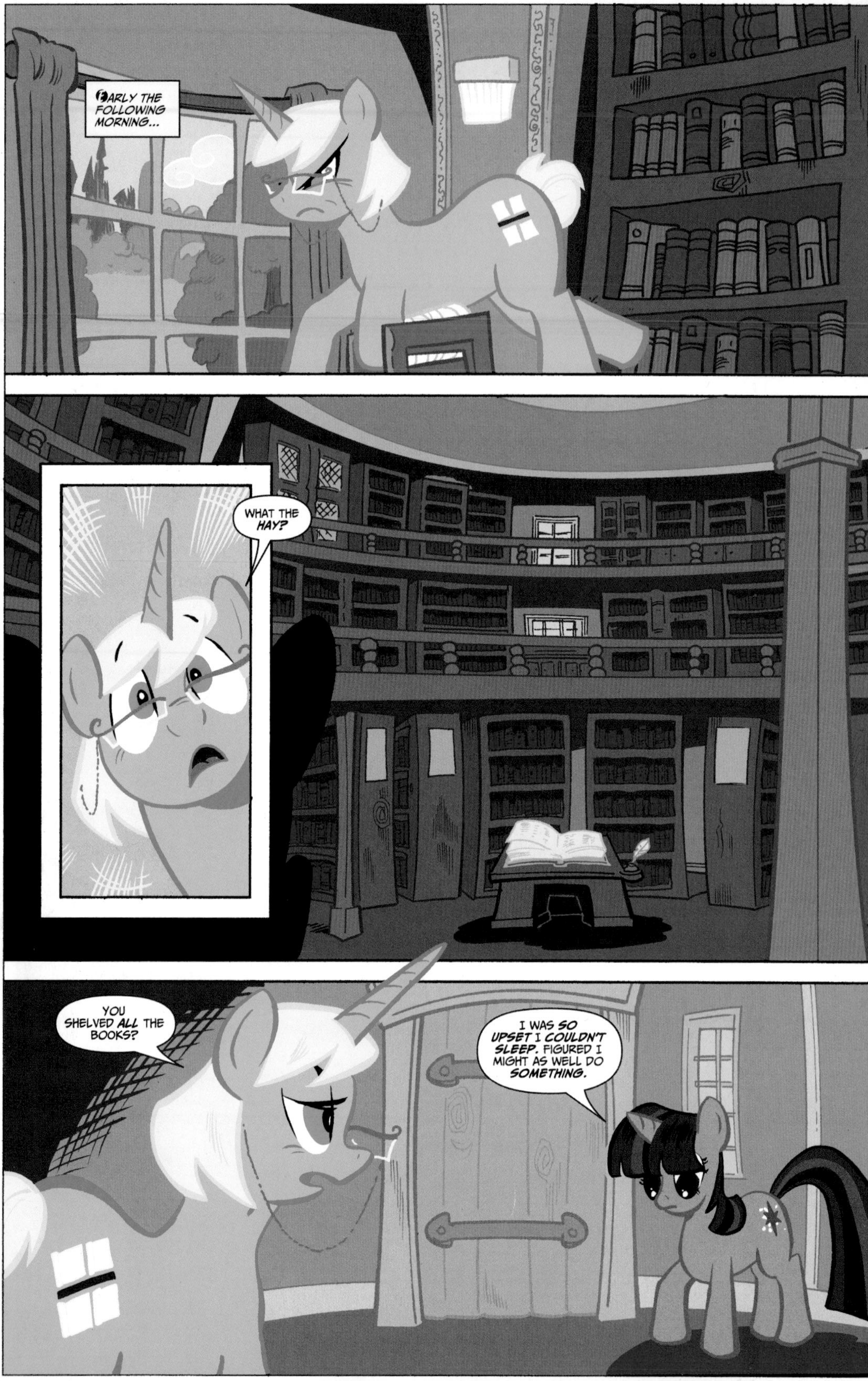
EARLY THE FOLLOWING MORNING...
WHAT THE *HAY?*
YOU SHELVED ***ALL*** THE BOOKS?
I WAS ***SO UPSET*** I ***COULDN'T SLEEP***. FIGURED I MIGHT AS WELL DO ***SOMETHING***.

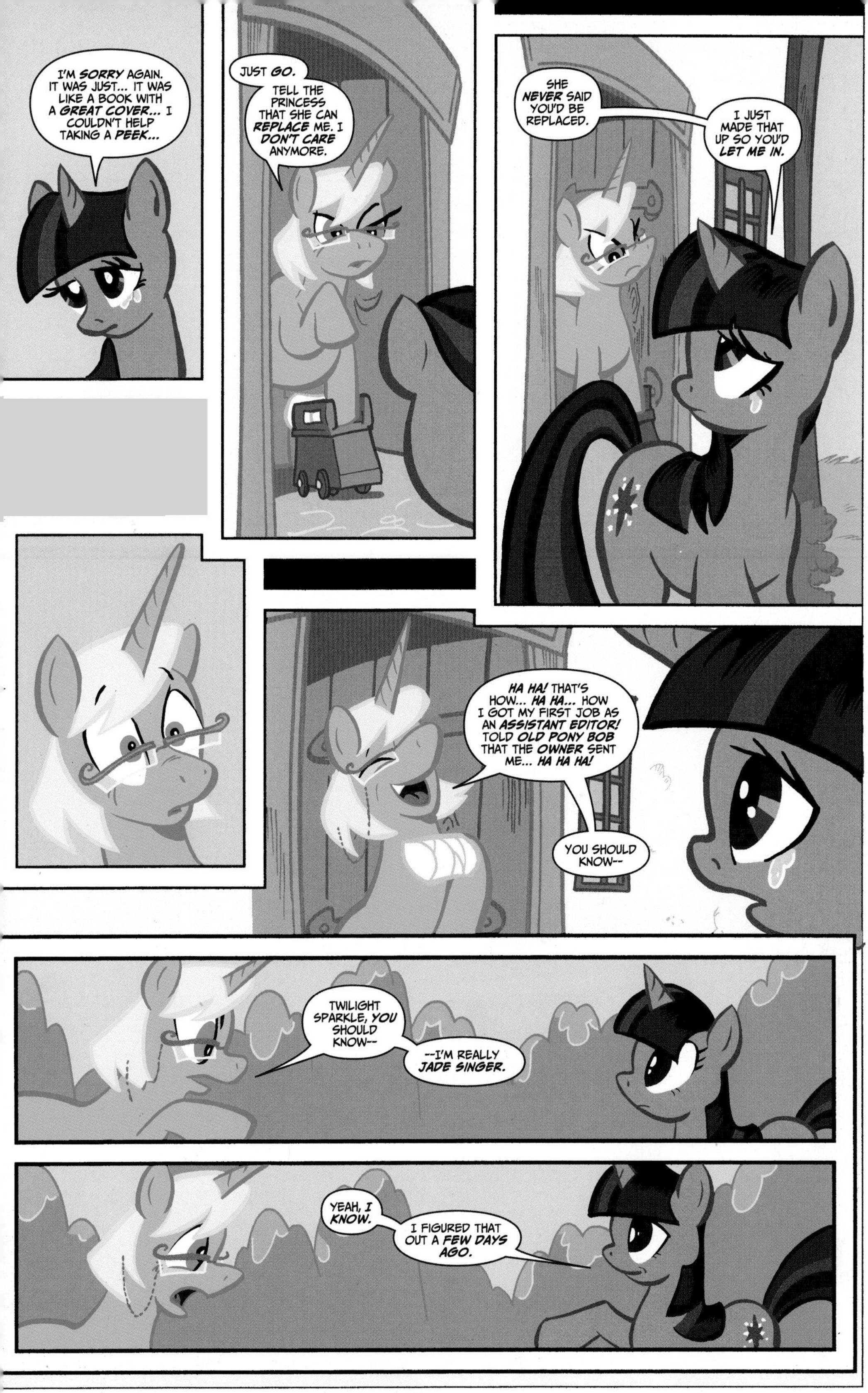
I'M SORRY AGAIN. IT WAS JUST... IT WAS LIKE A BOOK WITH A GREAT COVER... I COULDN'T HELP TAKING A PEEK...
JUST GO.
TELL THE PRINCESS THAT SHE CAN REPLACE ME. I DON'T CARE ANYMORE.
SHE NEVER SAID YOU'D BE REPLACED.
I JUST MADE THAT UP SO YOU'D LET ME IN.
HA HA! THAT'S HOW... HA HA... HOW I GOT MY FIRST JOB AS AN ASSISTANT EDITOR! TOLD OLD PONY BOB THAT THE OWNER SENT ME... HA HA HA!
YOU SHOULD KNOW--
TWILIGHT SPARKLE, YOU SHOULD KNOW--
--I'M REALLY JADE SINGER.
YEAH, I KNOW.
I FIGURED THAT OUT A FEW DAYS AGO.

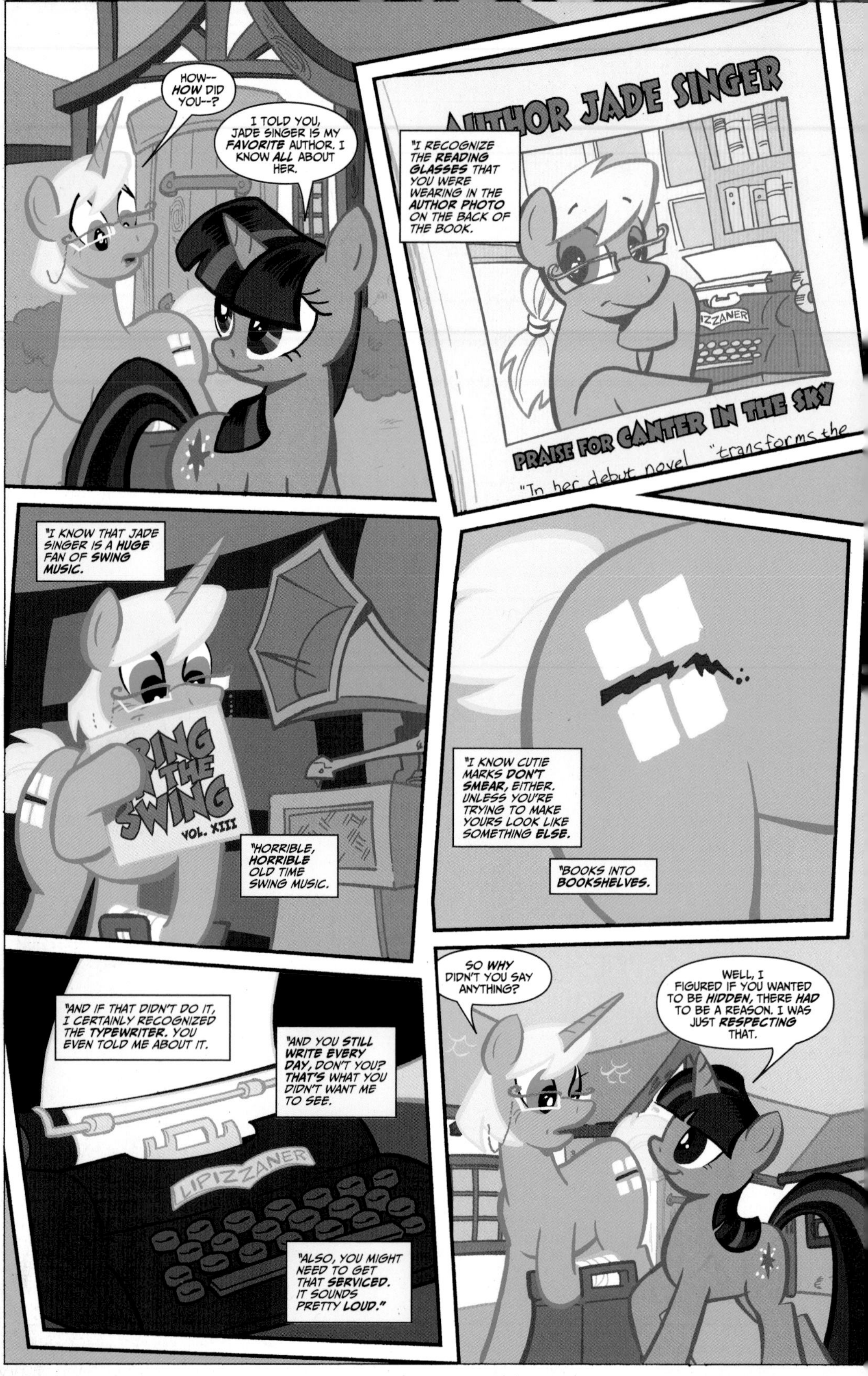

HOW-- HOW DID YOU--?
I TOLD YOU, JADE SINGER IS MY FAVORITE AUTHOR. I KNOW ALL ABOUT HER.
AUTHOR JADE SINGER
"I RECOGNIZE THE READING GLASSES THAT YOU WERE WEARING IN THE AUTHOR PHOTO ON THE BACK OF THE BOOK.
IZZANER
PRAISE FOR CANTER IN THE SKY
"In her debut novel
"transforms the
"I KNOW THAT JADE SINGER IS A HUGE FAN OF SWING MUSIC.
RING THE SWING VOL. XIII
"HORRIBLE, HORRIBLE OLD TIME SWING MUSIC.
"I KNOW CUTIE MARKS DON'T SMEAR, EITHER. UNLESS YOU'RE TRYING TO MAKE YOURS LOOK LIKE SOMETHING ELSE.
"BOOKS INTO BOOKSHELVES.
"AND IF THAT DIDN'T DO IT, I CERTAINLY RECOGNIZED THE TYPEWRITER. YOU EVEN TOLD ME ABOUT IT.
"AND YOU STILL WRITE EVERY DAY, DON'T YOU? THAT'S WHAT YOU DIDN'T WANT ME TO SEE.
LIPIZZANER
"ALSO, YOU MIGHT NEED TO GET THAT SERVICED. IT SOUNDS PRETTY LOUD."
SO WHY DIDN'T YOU SAY ANYTHING?
WELL, I FIGURED IF YOU WANTED TO BE HIDDEN, THERE HAD TO BE A REASON. I WAS JUST RESPECTING THAT.

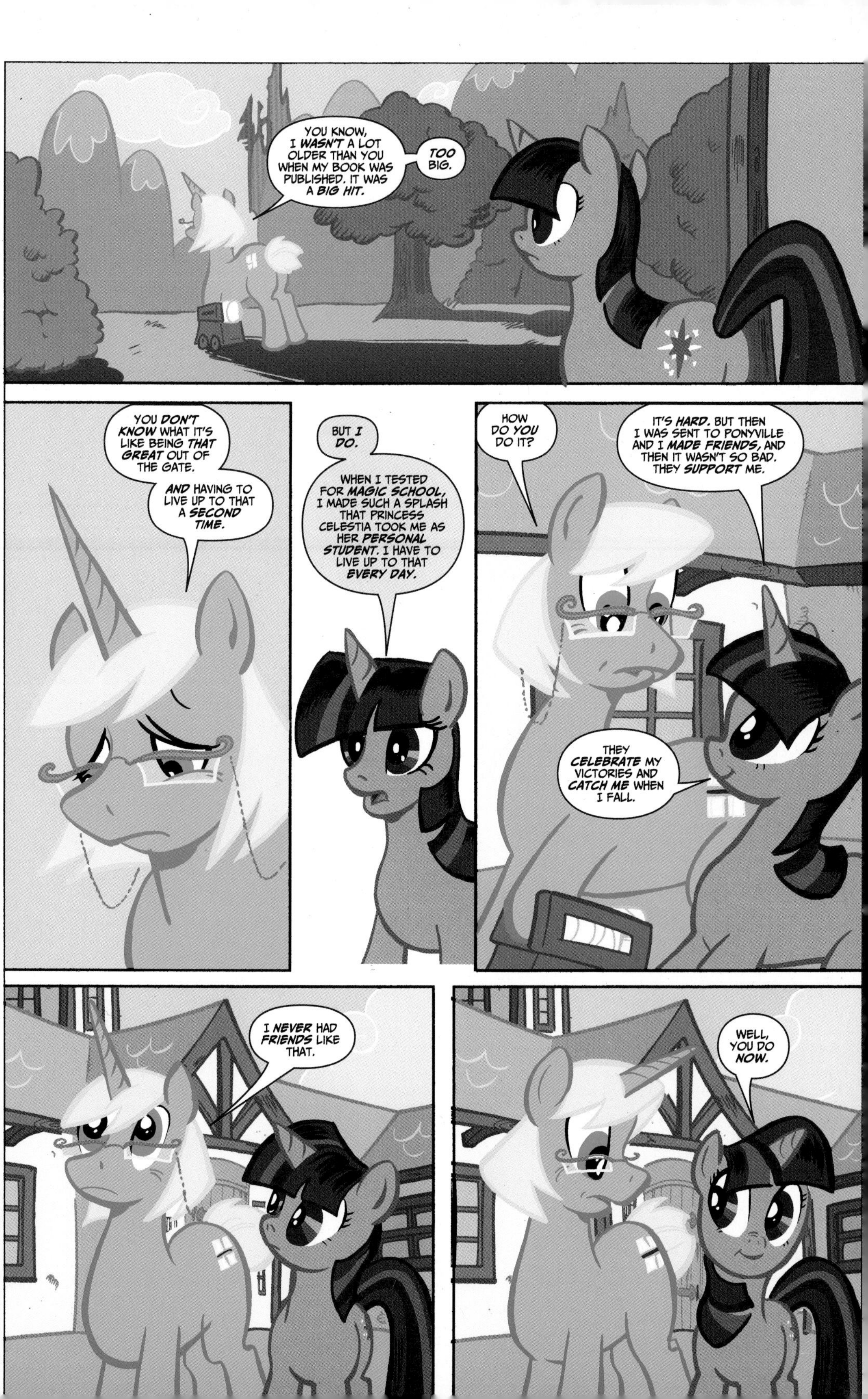
YOU KNOW, I WASN'T A LOT OLDER THAN YOU WHEN MY BOOK WAS PUBLISHED. IT WAS A BIG HIT.
TOO BIG.
YOU DON'T KNOW WHAT IT'S LIKE BEING THAT GREAT OUT OF THE GATE.
AND HAVING TO LIVE UP TO THAT A SECOND TIME.
BUT I DO.
WHEN I TESTED FOR MAGIC SCHOOL, I MADE SUCH A SPLASH THAT PRINCESS CELESTIA TOOK ME AS HER PERSONAL STUDENT. I HAVE TO LIVE UP TO THAT EVERY DAY.
HOW DO YOU DO IT?
IT'S HARD. BUT THEN I WAS SENT TO PONYVILLE AND I MADE FRIENDS, AND THEN IT WASN'T SO BAD. THEY SUPPORT ME.
THEY CELEBRATE MY VICTORIES AND CATCH ME WHEN I FALL.
I NEVER HAD FRIENDS LIKE THAT.
WELL, YOU DO NOW.

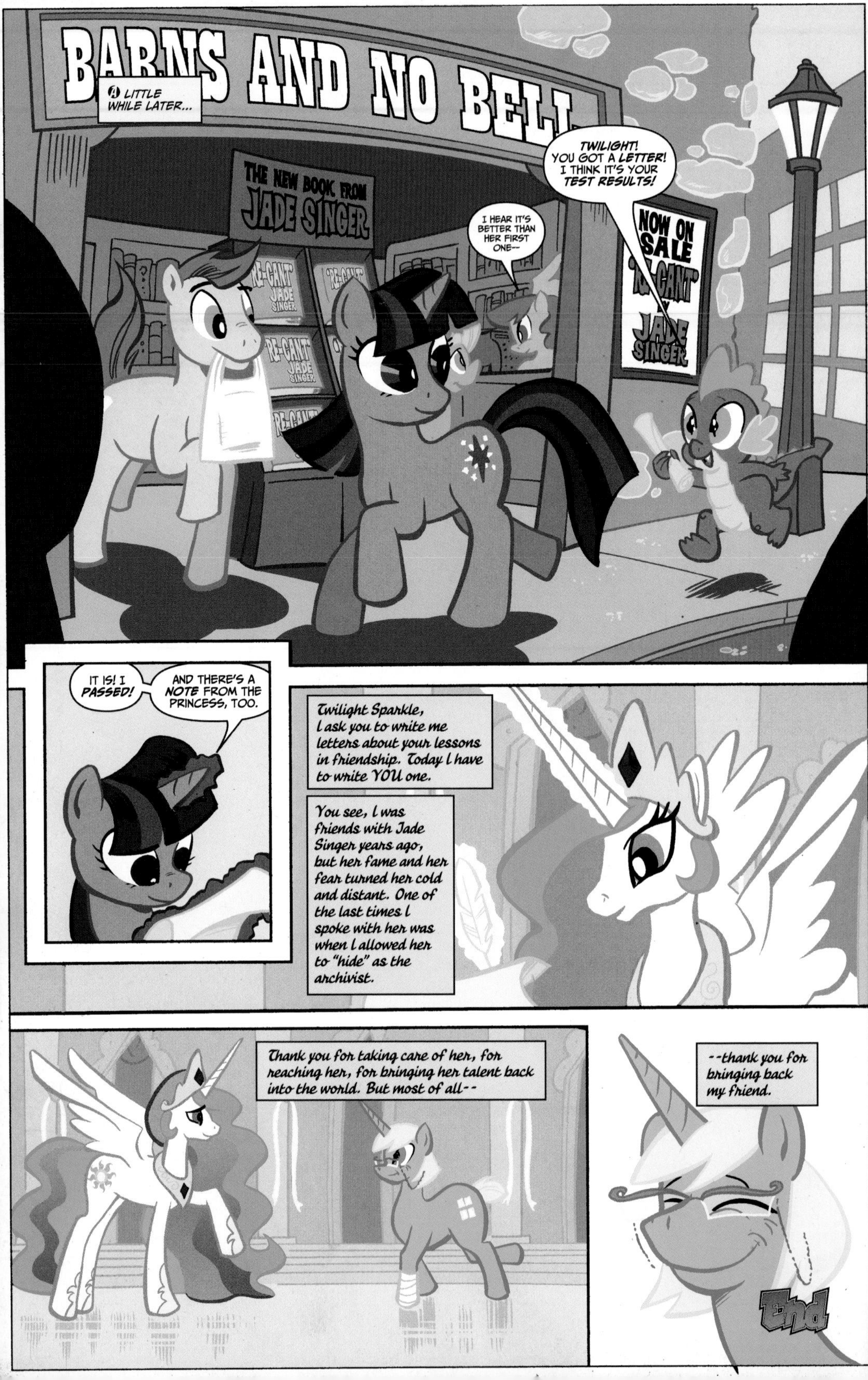
BARNS AND NO BELL
A LITTLE WHILE LATER...
THE NEW BOOK FROM JADE SINGER
RE-CANT JADE SINGER
NOW ON SALE "RE-CANT" BY JADE SINGER
I HEAR IT'S BETTER THAN HER FIRST ONE--
TWILIGHT! YOU GOT A LETTER! I THINK IT'S YOUR TEST RESULTS!
IT IS! I PASSED!
AND THERE'S A NOTE FROM THE PRINCESS, TOO.
Twilight Sparkle, I ask you to write me letters about your lessons in friendship. Today I have to write YOU one.
You see, I was friends with Jade Singer years ago, but her fame and her fear turned her cold and distant. One of the last times I spoke with her was when I allowed her to "hide" as the archivist.
Thank you for taking care of her, for reaching her, for bringing her talent back into the world. But most of all--
--thank you for bringing back my friend.
End

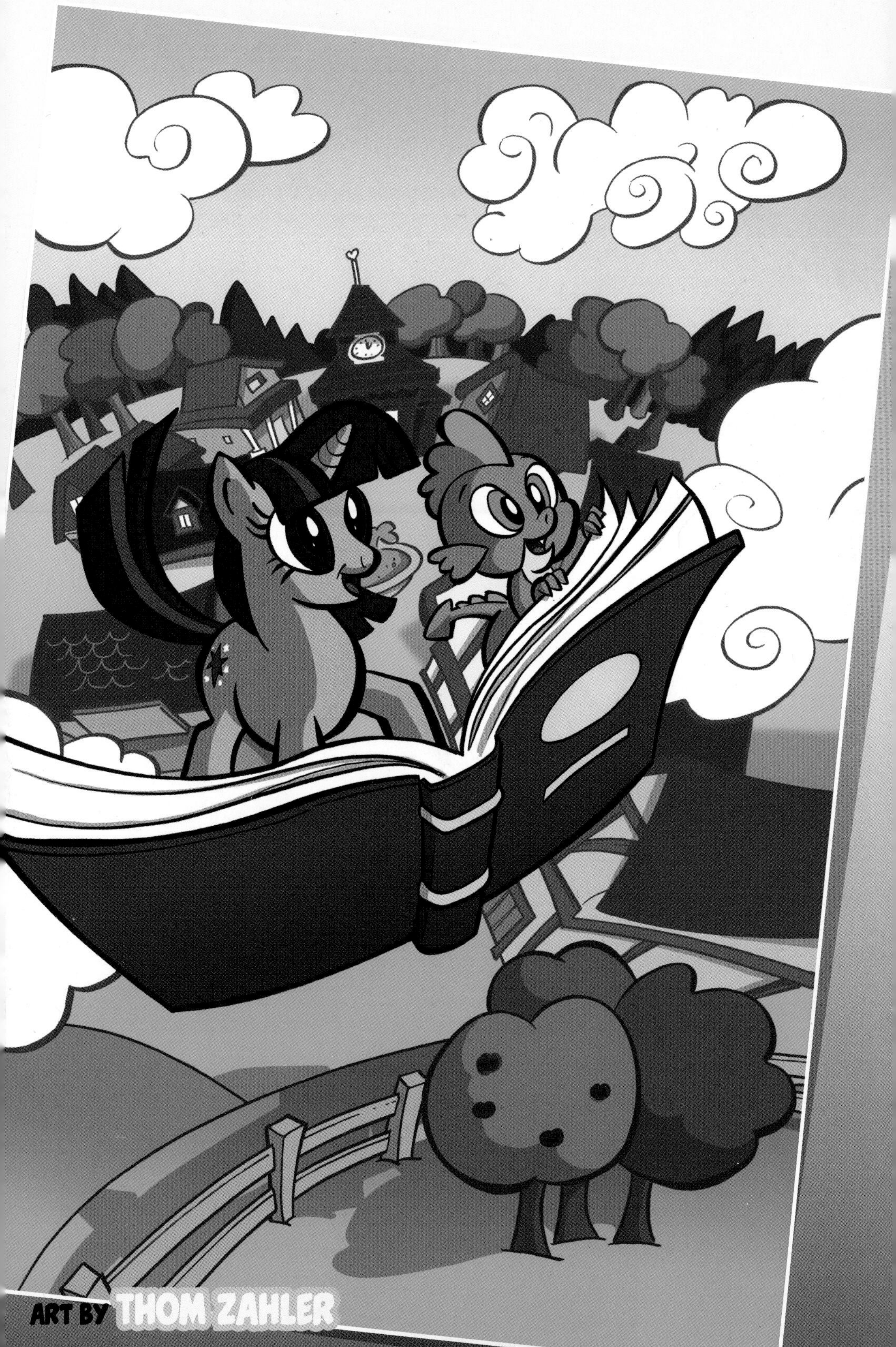

ART BY THOM ZAHLER

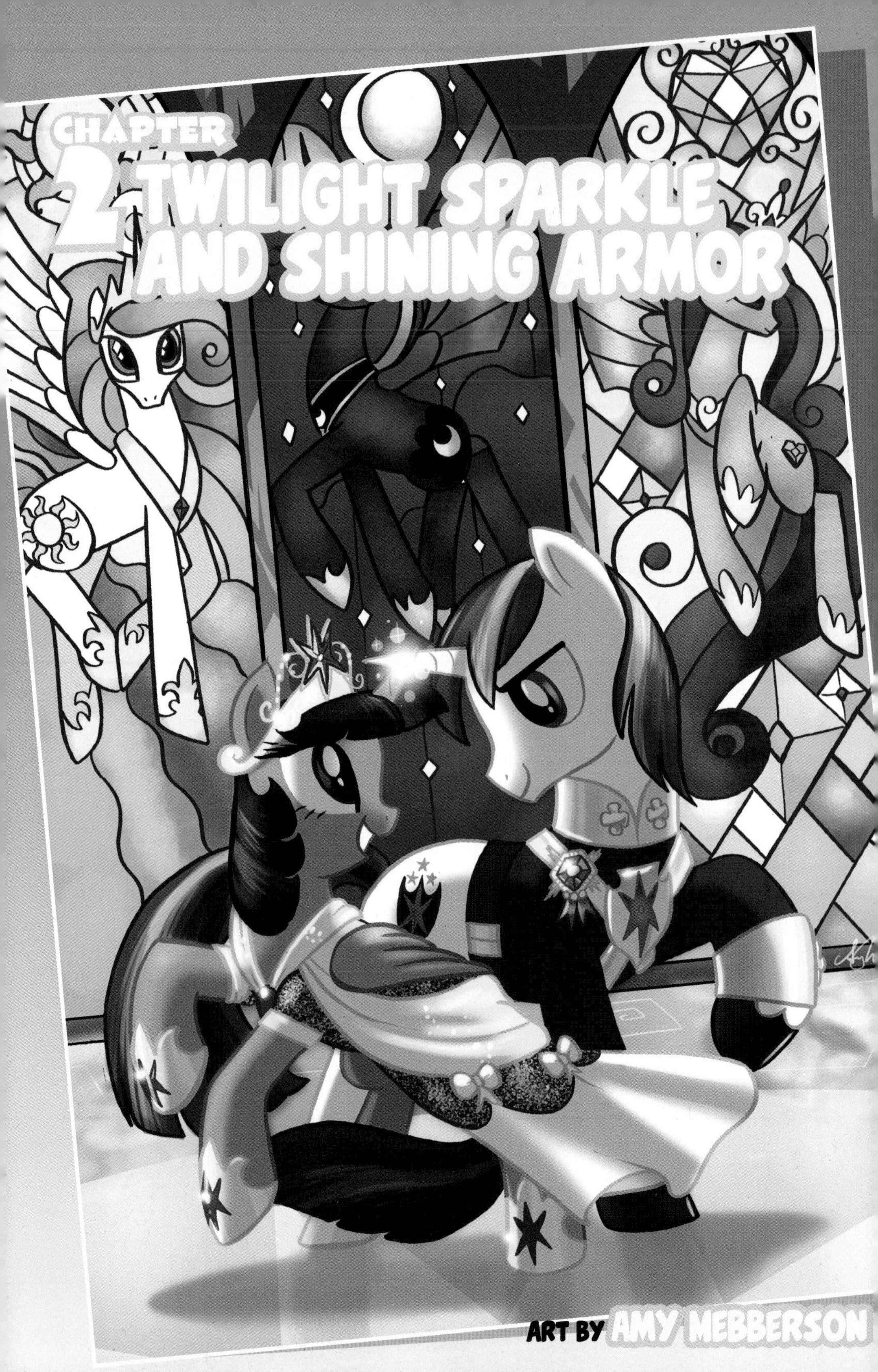
CHAPTER 2
TWILIGHT SPARKLE AND SHINING ARMOR
ART BY AMY MEBBERSON

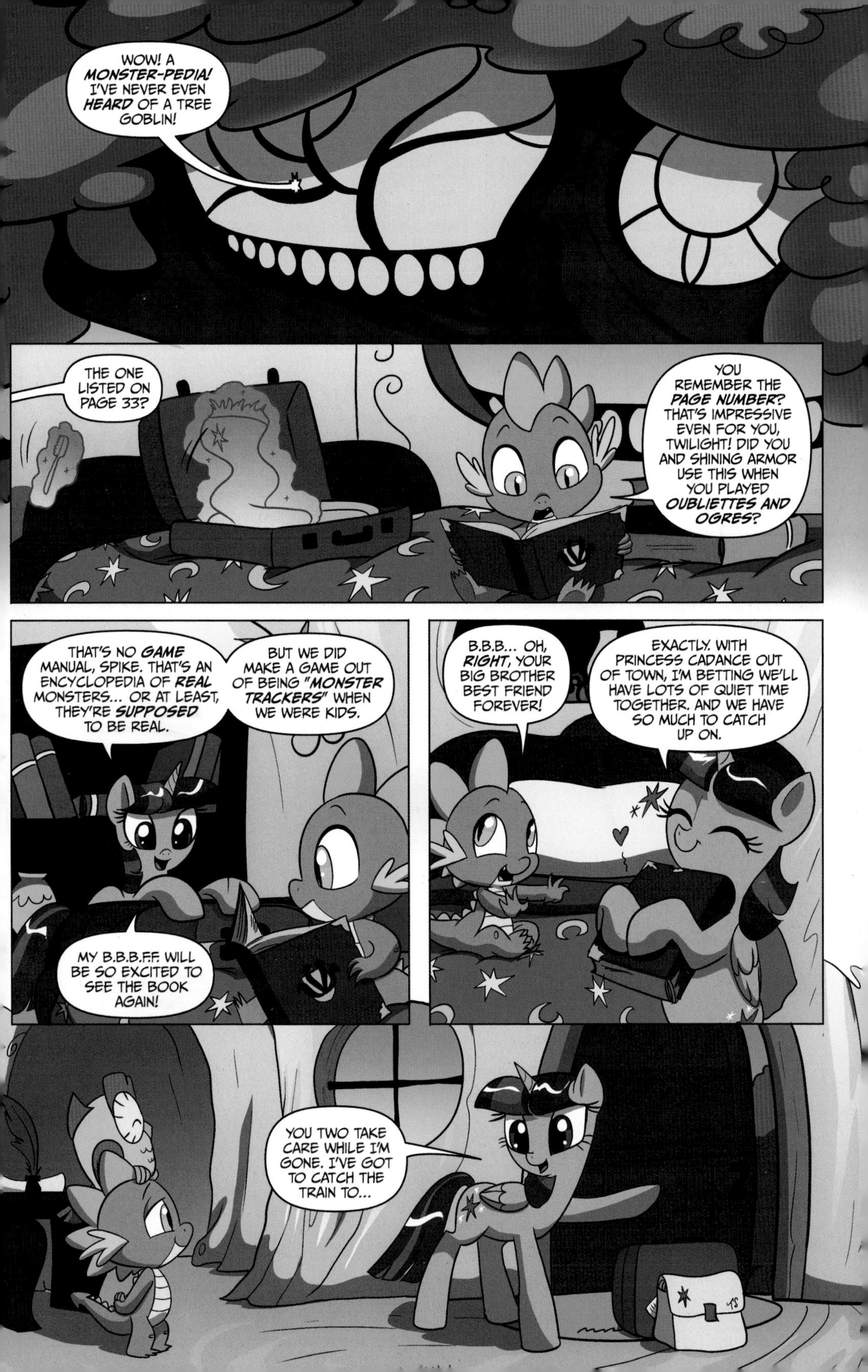

WOW! A MONSTER-PEDIA! I'VE NEVER EVEN HEARD OF A TREE GOBLIN!
THE ONE LISTED ON PAGE 33?
YOU REMEMBER THE PAGE NUMBER? THAT'S IMPRESSIVE EVEN FOR YOU, TWILIGHT! DID YOU AND SHINING ARMOR USE THIS WHEN YOU PLAYED OUBLIETTES AND OGRES?
THAT'S NO GAME MANUAL, SPIKE. THAT'S AN ENCYCLOPEDIA OF REAL MONSTERS... OR AT LEAST, THEY'RE SUPPOSED TO BE REAL.
BUT WE DID MAKE A GAME OUT OF BEING "MONSTER TRACKERS" WHEN WE WERE KIDS.
MY B.B.B.F.F. WILL BE SO EXCITED TO SEE THE BOOK AGAIN!
B.B.B... OH, RIGHT, YOUR BIG BROTHER BEST FRIEND FOREVER!
EXACTLY. WITH PRINCESS CADANCE OUT OF TOWN, I'M BETTING WE'LL HAVE LOTS OF QUIET TIME TOGETHER. AND WE HAVE SO MUCH TO CATCH UP ON.
YOU TWO TAKE CARE WHILE I'M GONE. I'VE GOT TO CATCH THE TRAIN TO...

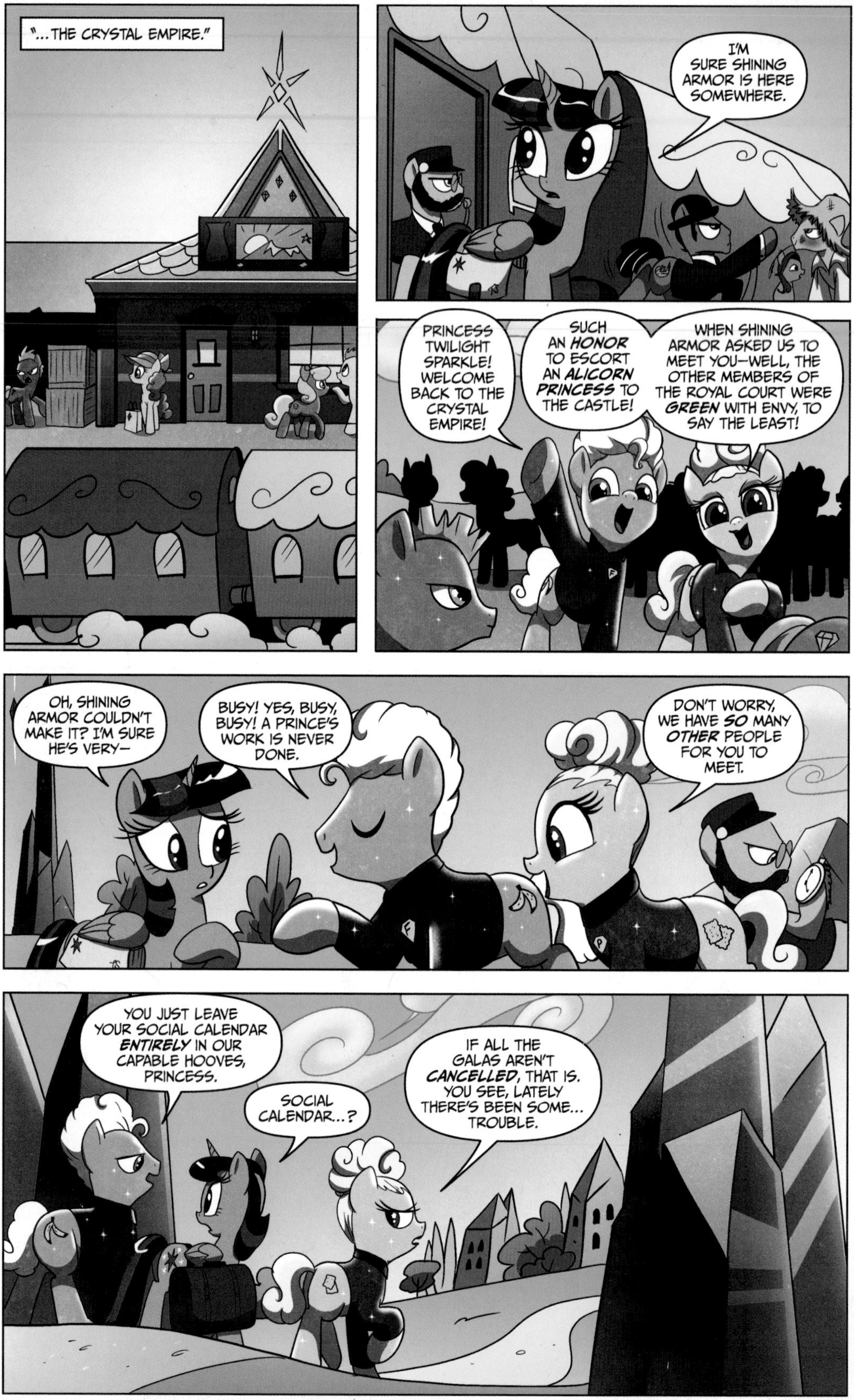
"...THE CRYSTAL EMPIRE."
I'M SURE SHINING ARMOR IS HERE SOMEWHERE.
PRINCESS TWILIGHT SPARKLE! WELCOME BACK TO THE CRYSTAL EMPIRE!
SUCH AN HONOR TO ESCORT AN ALICORN PRINCESS TO THE CASTLE!
WHEN SHINING ARMOR ASKED US TO MEET YOU—WELL, THE OTHER MEMBERS OF THE ROYAL COURT WERE GREEN WITH ENVY, TO SAY THE LEAST!
OH, SHINING ARMOR COULDN'T MAKE IT? I'M SURE HE'S VERY—
BUSY! YES, BUSY, BUSY! A PRINCE'S WORK IS NEVER DONE.
DON'T WORRY, WE HAVE SO MANY OTHER PEOPLE FOR YOU TO MEET.
YOU JUST LEAVE YOUR SOCIAL CALENDAR ENTIRELY IN OUR CAPABLE HOOVES, PRINCESS.
SOCIAL CALENDAR...?
IF ALL THE GALAS AREN'T CANCELLED, THAT IS. YOU SEE, LATELY THERE'S BEEN SOME... TROUBLE.

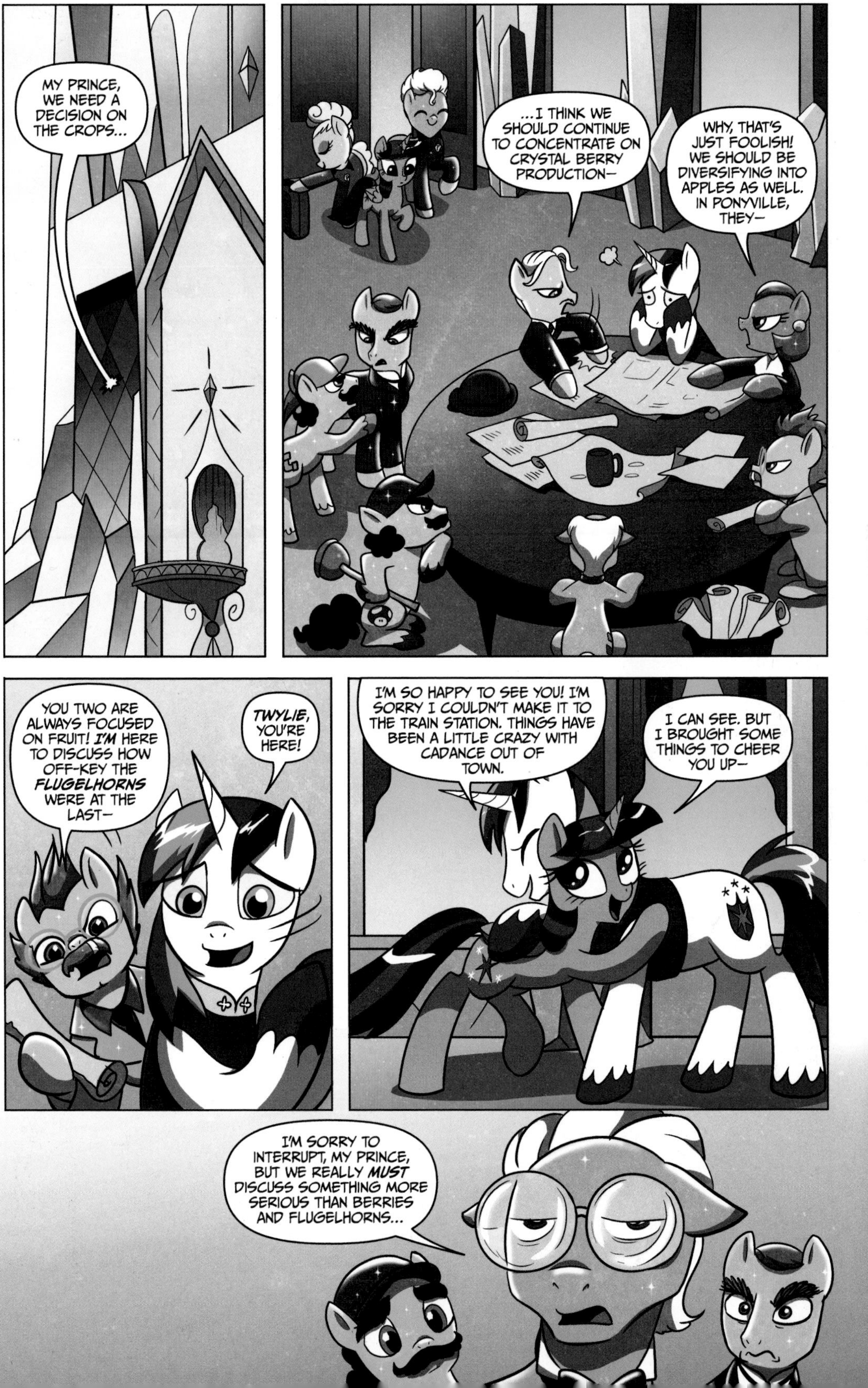
MY PRINCE, WE NEED A DECISION ON THE CROPS...
...I THINK WE SHOULD CONTINUE TO CONCENTRATE ON CRYSTAL BERRY PRODUCTION—
WHY, THAT'S JUST FOOLISH! WE SHOULD BE DIVERSIFYING INTO APPLES AS WELL. IN PONYVILLE, THEY—
YOU TWO ARE ALWAYS FOCUSED ON FRUIT! *I'M* HERE TO DISCUSS HOW OFF-KEY THE ***FLUGELHORNS*** WERE AT THE LAST—
TWYLIE, YOU'RE HERE!
I'M SO HAPPY TO SEE YOU! I'M SORRY I COULDN'T MAKE IT TO THE TRAIN STATION. THINGS HAVE BEEN A LITTLE CRAZY WITH CADANCE OUT OF TOWN.
I CAN SEE. BUT I BROUGHT SOME THINGS TO CHEER YOU UP—
I'M SORRY TO INTERRUPT, MY PRINCE, BUT WE REALLY ***MUST*** DISCUSS SOMETHING MORE SERIOUS THAN BERRIES AND FLUGELHORNS...

...NAMELY, THE **STRANGE OCCURRENCES** THAT CONTINUE THROUGHOUT THE CASTLE, AND ESPECIALLY IN MY LIBRARY.

OH, NOT THIS AGAIN! HERE WE GO...

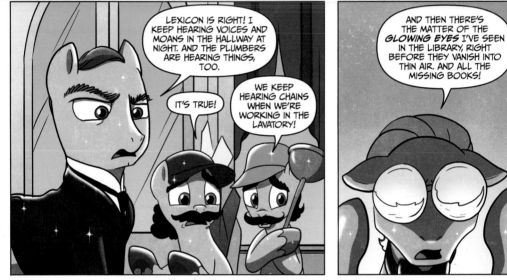

LEXICON IS RIGHT! I KEEP HEARING VOICES AND MOANS IN THE HALLWAY AT NIGHT. AND THE PLUMBERS ARE HEARING THINGS, TOO.

IT'S TRUE!

WE KEEP HEARING CHAINS WHEN WE'RE WORKING IN THE LAVATORY!

AND THEN THERE'S THE MATTER OF THE **GLOWING EYES** I'VE SEEN IN THE LIBRARY, RIGHT BEFORE THEY VANISH INTO THIN AIR. AND ALL THE MISSING BOOKS!

I'M SO SORRY TO RAISE THIS DURING YOUR VISIT, PRINCESS CELESTIA.

UH... I'M NOT CELES—

LEX, YOU DID PROMISE TO GET YOUR EYES CHECKED AGAIN, RIGHT?

HOLD ON, BIG BROTHER. LOOK WHAT I BROUGHT!

DOESN'T THIS ALL SOUND FAMILIAR? MOANS IN THE DARK? GLOWING EYES. DRAGGING CHAINS. AND **STEALING BOOKS!**

IT SOUNDS JUST LIKE A **CRYSTAL GHOST**—ON **PAGE 89!**

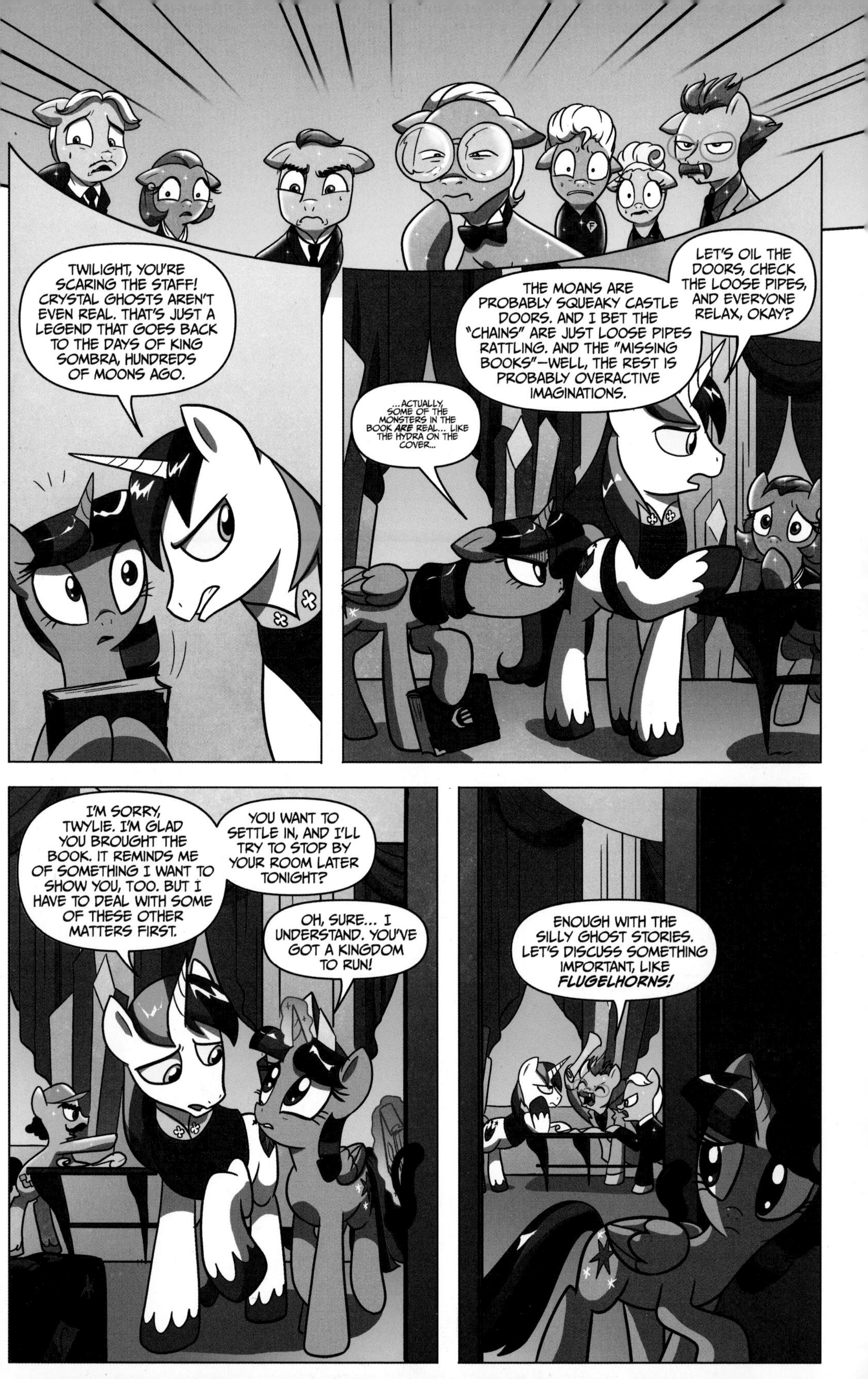
TWILIGHT, YOU'RE SCARING THE STAFF! CRYSTAL GHOSTS AREN'T EVEN REAL. THAT'S JUST A LEGEND THAT GOES BACK TO THE DAYS OF KING SOMBRA, HUNDREDS OF MOONS AGO.
THE MOANS ARE PROBABLY SQUEAKY CASTLE DOORS. AND I BET THE "CHAINS" ARE JUST LOOSE PIPES RATTLING. AND THE "MISSING BOOKS"—WELL, THE REST IS PROBABLY OVERACTIVE IMAGINATIONS.
LET'S OIL THE DOORS, CHECK THE LOOSE PIPES, AND EVERYONE RELAX, OKAY?
...ACTUALLY, SOME OF THE MONSTERS IN THE BOOK *ARE* REAL... LIKE THE HYDRA ON THE COVER...
I'M SORRY, TWYLIE. I'M GLAD YOU BROUGHT THE BOOK. IT REMINDS ME OF SOMETHING I WANT TO SHOW YOU, TOO. BUT I HAVE TO DEAL WITH SOME OF THESE OTHER MATTERS FIRST.
YOU WANT TO SETTLE IN, AND I'LL TRY TO STOP BY YOUR ROOM LATER TONIGHT?
OH, SURE... I UNDERSTAND. YOU'VE GOT A KINGDOM TO RUN!
ENOUGH WITH THE SILLY GHOST STORIES. LET'S DISCUSS SOMETHING IMPORTANT, LIKE ***FLUGELHORNS!***

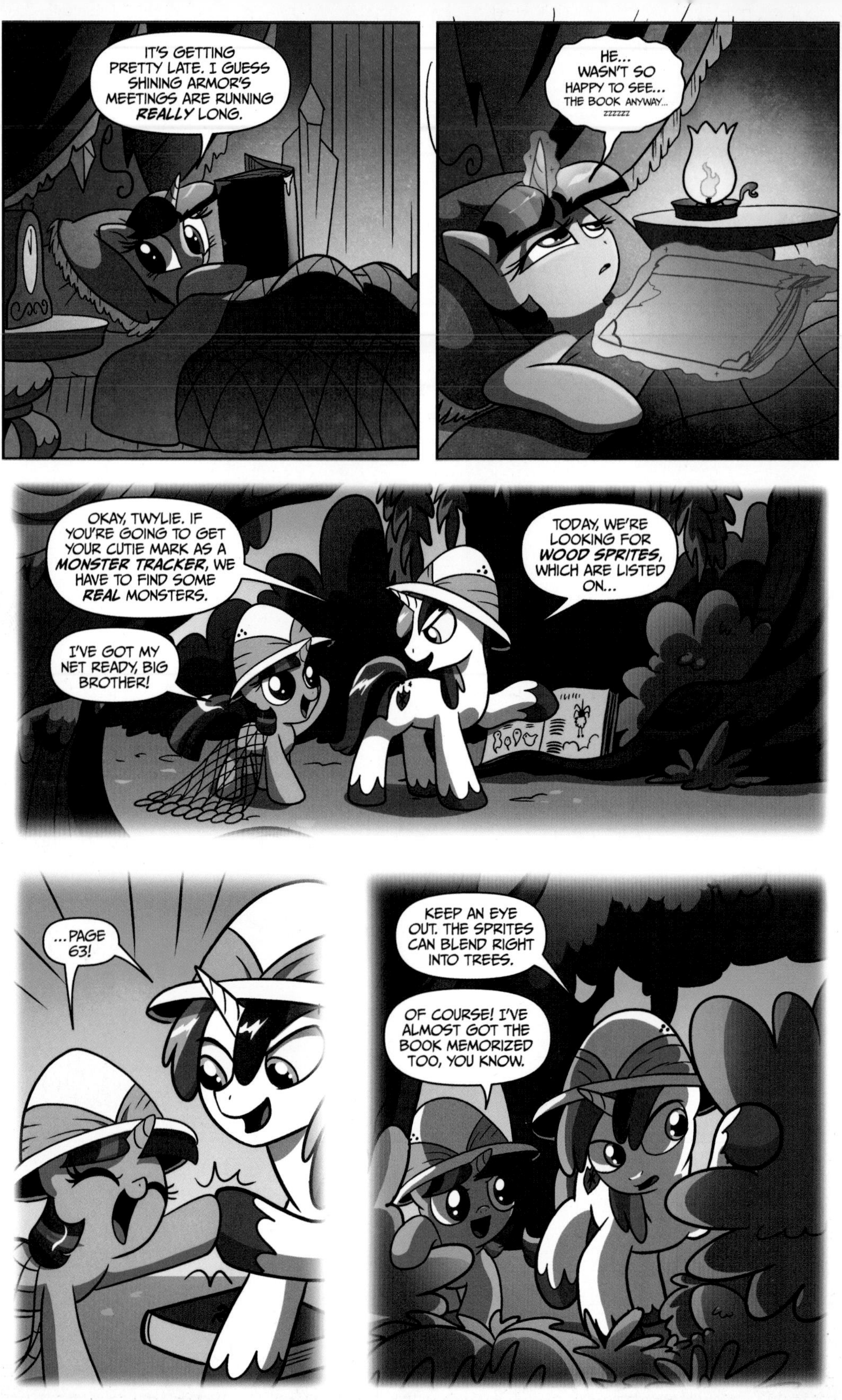
IT'S GETTING PRETTY LATE. I GUESS SHINING ARMOR'S MEETINGS ARE RUNNING REALLY LONG.
HE... WASN'T SO HAPPY TO SEE... THE BOOK ANYWAY... ZZZZZZ
OKAY, TWYLIE. IF YOU'RE GOING TO GET YOUR CUTIE MARK AS A MONSTER TRACKER, WE HAVE TO FIND SOME REAL MONSTERS.
I'VE GOT MY NET READY, BIG BROTHER!
TODAY, WE'RE LOOKING FOR WOOD SPRITES, WHICH ARE LISTED ON...
...PAGE 63!
KEEP AN EYE OUT. THE SPRITES CAN BLEND RIGHT INTO TREES.
OF COURSE! I'VE ALMOST GOT THE BOOK MEMORIZED TOO, YOU KNOW.

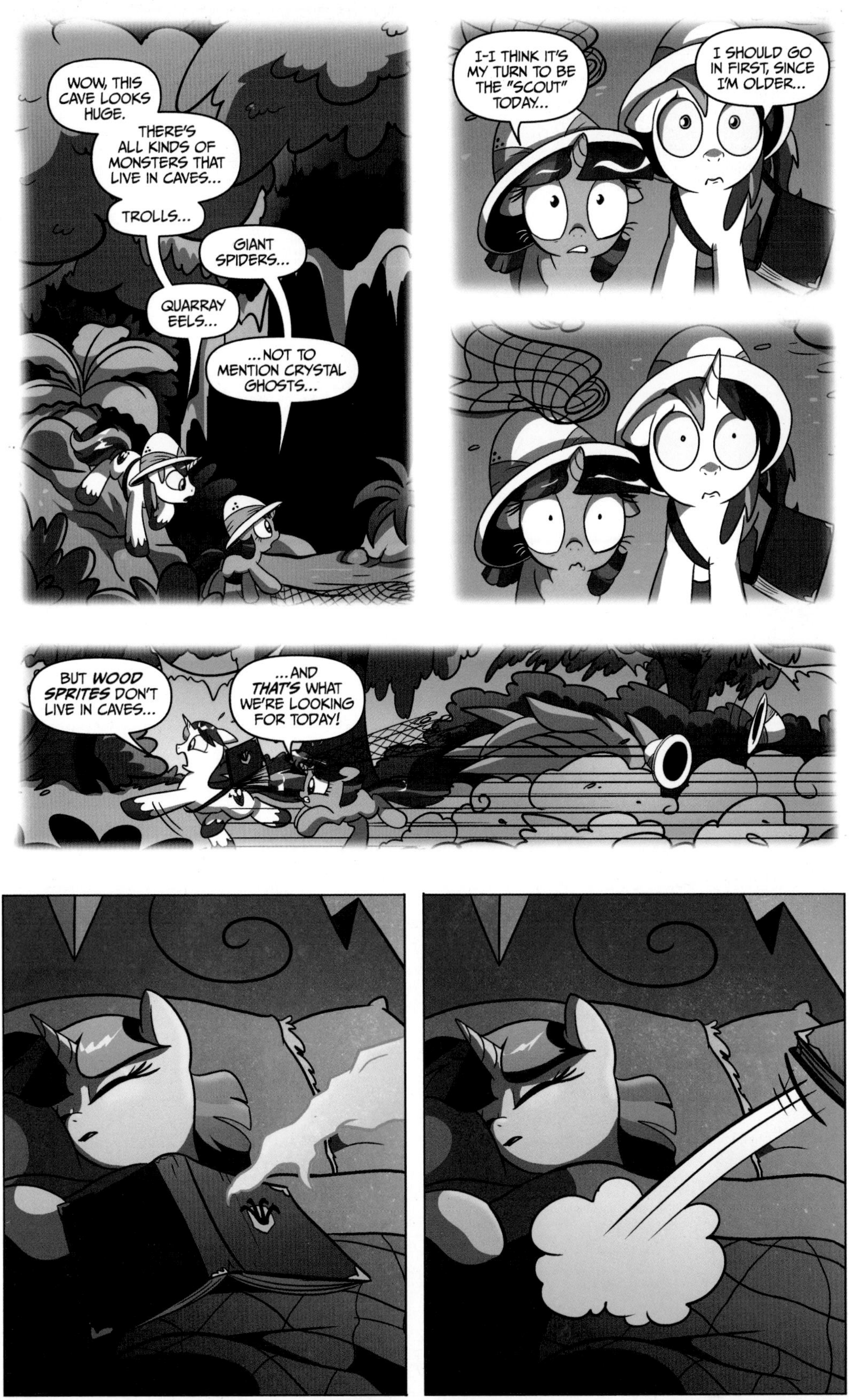
WOW, THIS CAVE LOOKS HUGE.
THERE'S ALL KINDS OF MONSTERS THAT LIVE IN CAVES...
TROLLS...
GIANT SPIDERS...
QUARRAY EELS...
...NOT TO MENTION CRYSTAL GHOSTS...
I-I THINK IT'S MY TURN TO BE THE "SCOUT" TODAY...
I SHOULD GO IN FIRST, SINCE I'M OLDER...
BUT WOOD SPRITES DON'T LIVE IN CAVES...
...AND THAT'S WHAT WE'RE LOOKING FOR TODAY!

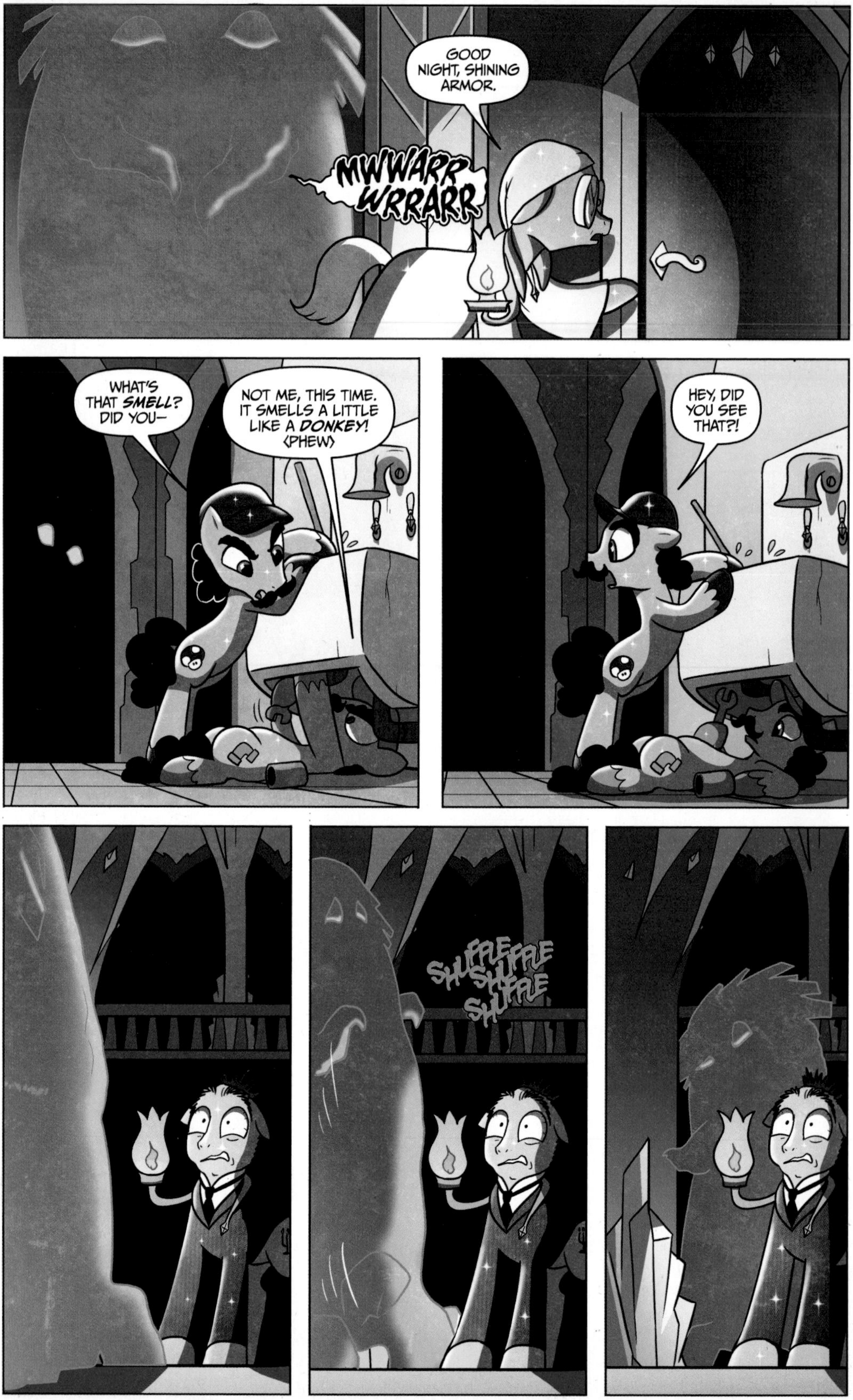
GOOD NIGHT, SHINING ARMOR.
MWWARR WRRARR
WHAT'S THAT SMELL? DID YOU—
NOT ME, THIS TIME. IT SMELLS A LITTLE LIKE A DONKEY! ‹PHEW›
HEY, DID YOU SEE THAT?!
SHUFFLE SHUFFLE SHUFFLE

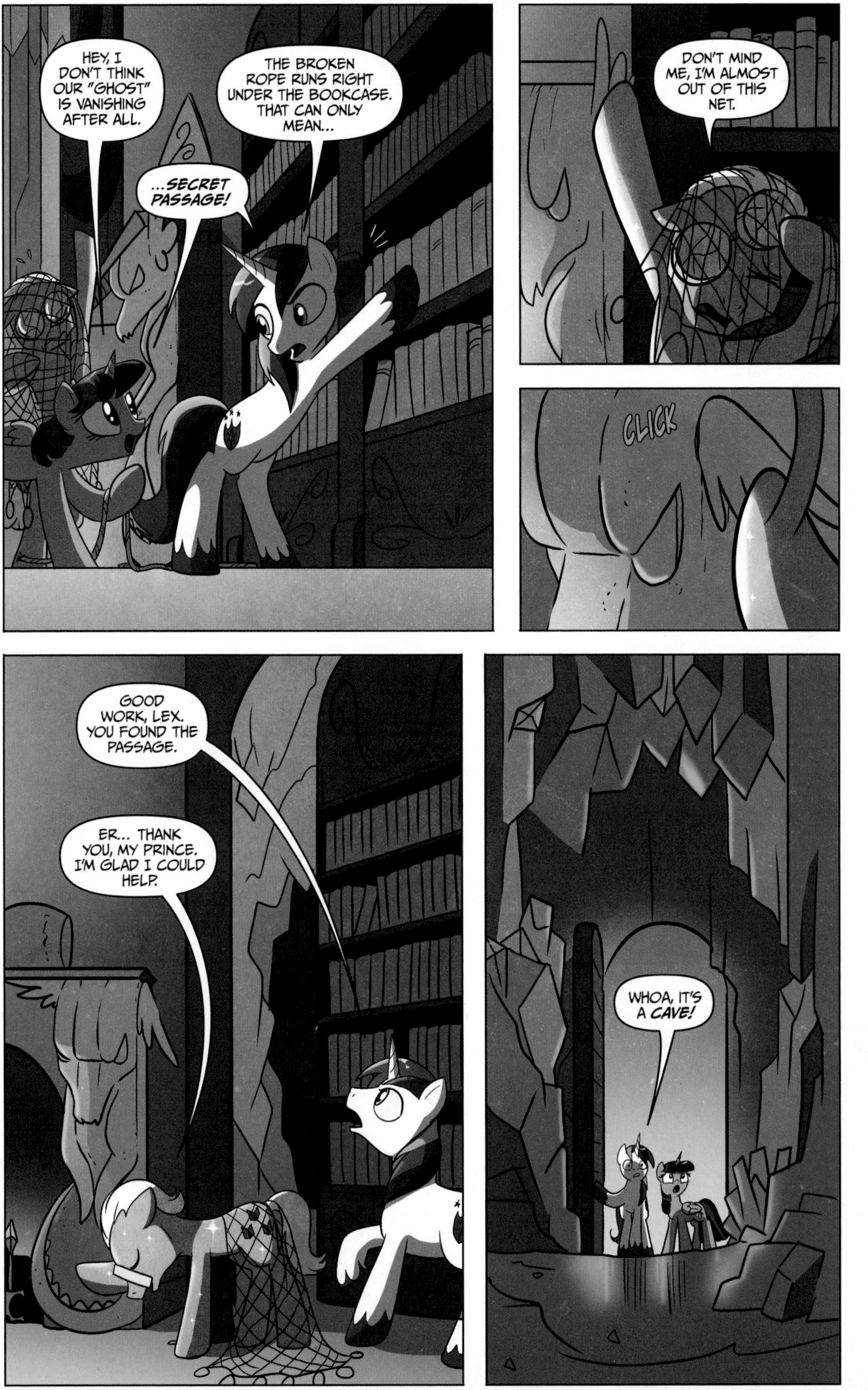
HEY, I DON'T THINK OUR "GHOST" IS VANISHING AFTER ALL.
THE BROKEN ROPE RUNS RIGHT UNDER THE BOOKCASE. THAT CAN ONLY MEAN...
...SECRET PASSAGE!
DON'T MIND ME, I'M ALMOST OUT OF THIS NET.
CLICK
GOOD WORK, LEX. YOU FOUND THE PASSAGE.
ER... THANK YOU, MY PRINCE. I'M GLAD I COULD HELP.
WHOA, IT'S A CAVE!

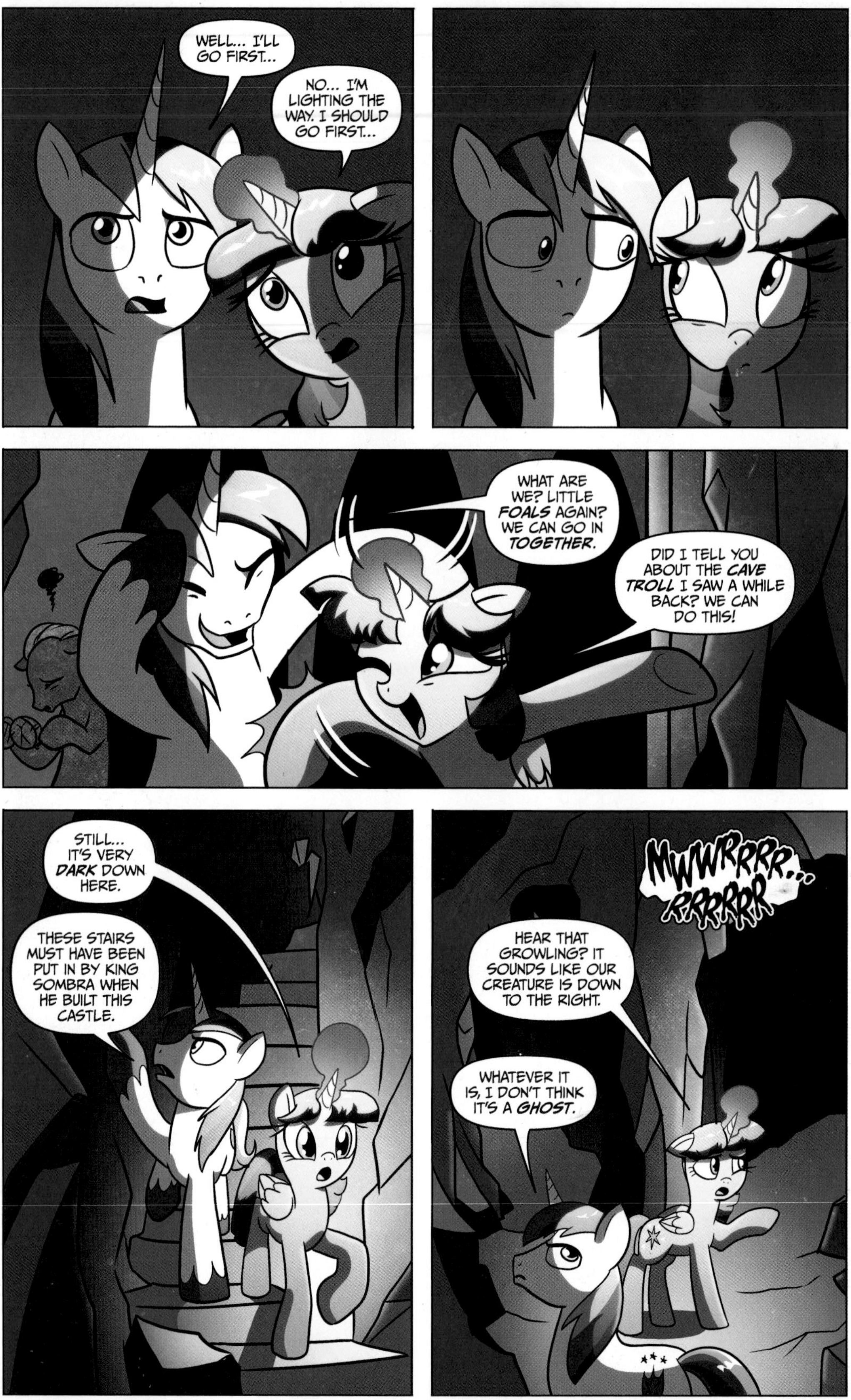
WELL... I'LL GO FIRST...
NO... I'M LIGHTING THE WAY. I SHOULD GO FIRST...
WHAT ARE WE? LITTLE *FOALS* AGAIN? WE CAN GO IN *TOGETHER*.
DID I TELL YOU ABOUT THE *CAVE TROLL* I SAW A WHILE BACK? WE CAN DO THIS!
STILL... IT'S VERY *DARK* DOWN HERE.
THESE STAIRS MUST HAVE BEEN PUT IN BY KING SOMBRA WHEN HE BUILT THIS CASTLE.
MWWRRRR... RRRRRR
HEAR THAT GROWLING? IT SOUNDS LIKE OUR CREATURE IS DOWN TO THE RIGHT.
WHATEVER IT IS, I DON'T THINK IT'S A *GHOST*.

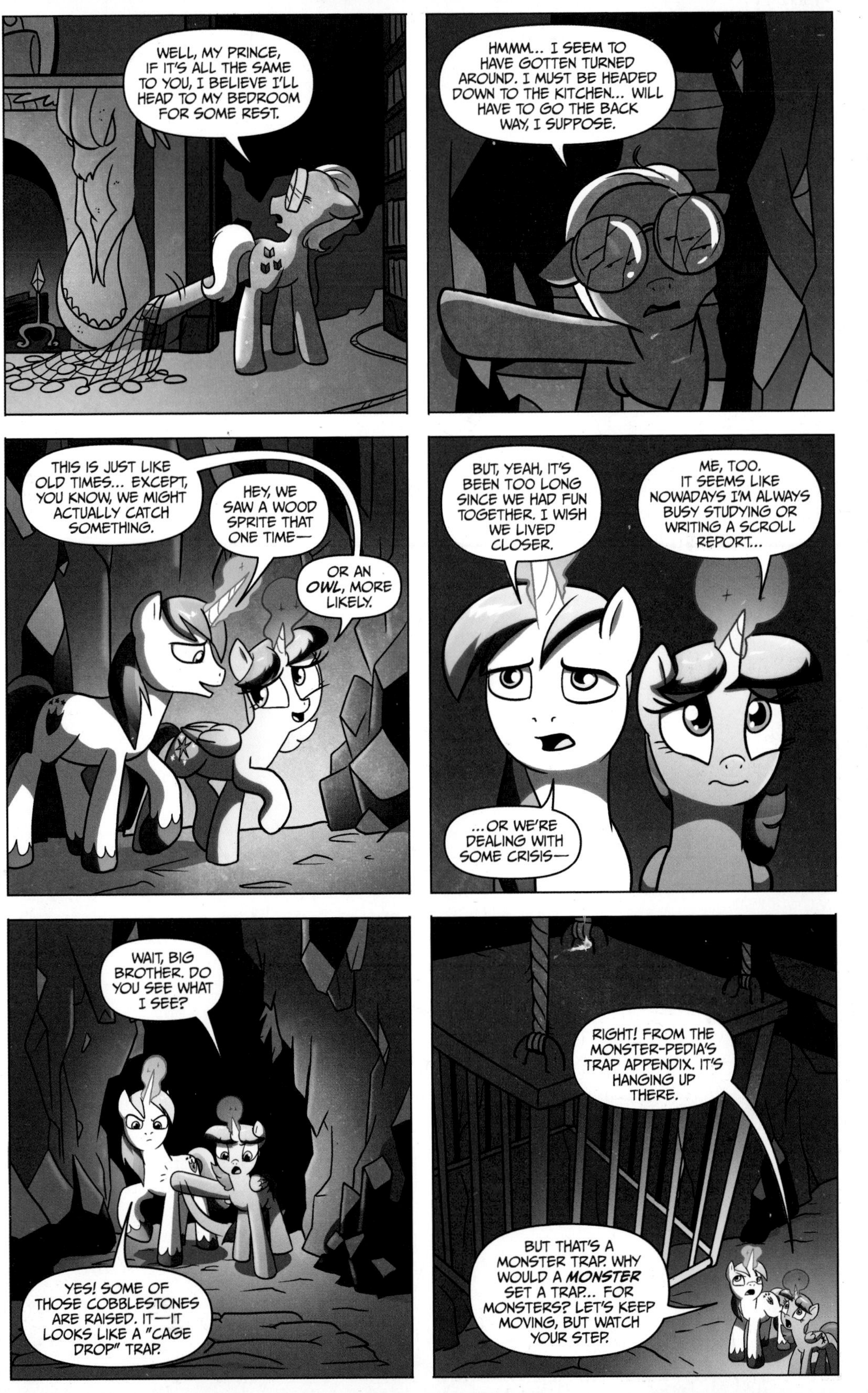
WELL, MY PRINCE, IF IT'S ALL THE SAME TO YOU, I BELIEVE I'LL HEAD TO MY BEDROOM FOR SOME REST.
HMMM... I SEEM TO HAVE GOTTEN TURNED AROUND. I MUST BE HEADED DOWN TO THE KITCHEN... WILL HAVE TO GO THE BACK WAY, I SUPPOSE.
THIS IS JUST LIKE OLD TIMES... EXCEPT, YOU KNOW, WE MIGHT ACTUALLY CATCH SOMETHING.
HEY, WE SAW A WOOD SPRITE THAT ONE TIME—
OR AN *OWL*, MORE LIKELY.
BUT, YEAH, IT'S BEEN TOO LONG SINCE WE HAD FUN TOGETHER. I WISH WE LIVED CLOSER.
ME, TOO. IT SEEMS LIKE NOWADAYS I'M ALWAYS BUSY STUDYING OR WRITING A SCROLL REPORT...
...OR WE'RE DEALING WITH SOME CRISIS—
WAIT, BIG BROTHER. DO YOU SEE WHAT I SEE?
YES! SOME OF THOSE COBBLESTONES ARE RAISED. IT—IT LOOKS LIKE A "CAGE DROP" TRAP.
RIGHT! FROM THE MONSTER-PEDIA'S TRAP APPENDIX. IT'S HANGING UP THERE.
BUT THAT'S A MONSTER TRAP. WHY WOULD A ***MONSTER*** SET A TRAP... FOR MONSTERS? LET'S KEEP MOVING, BUT WATCH YOUR STEP.

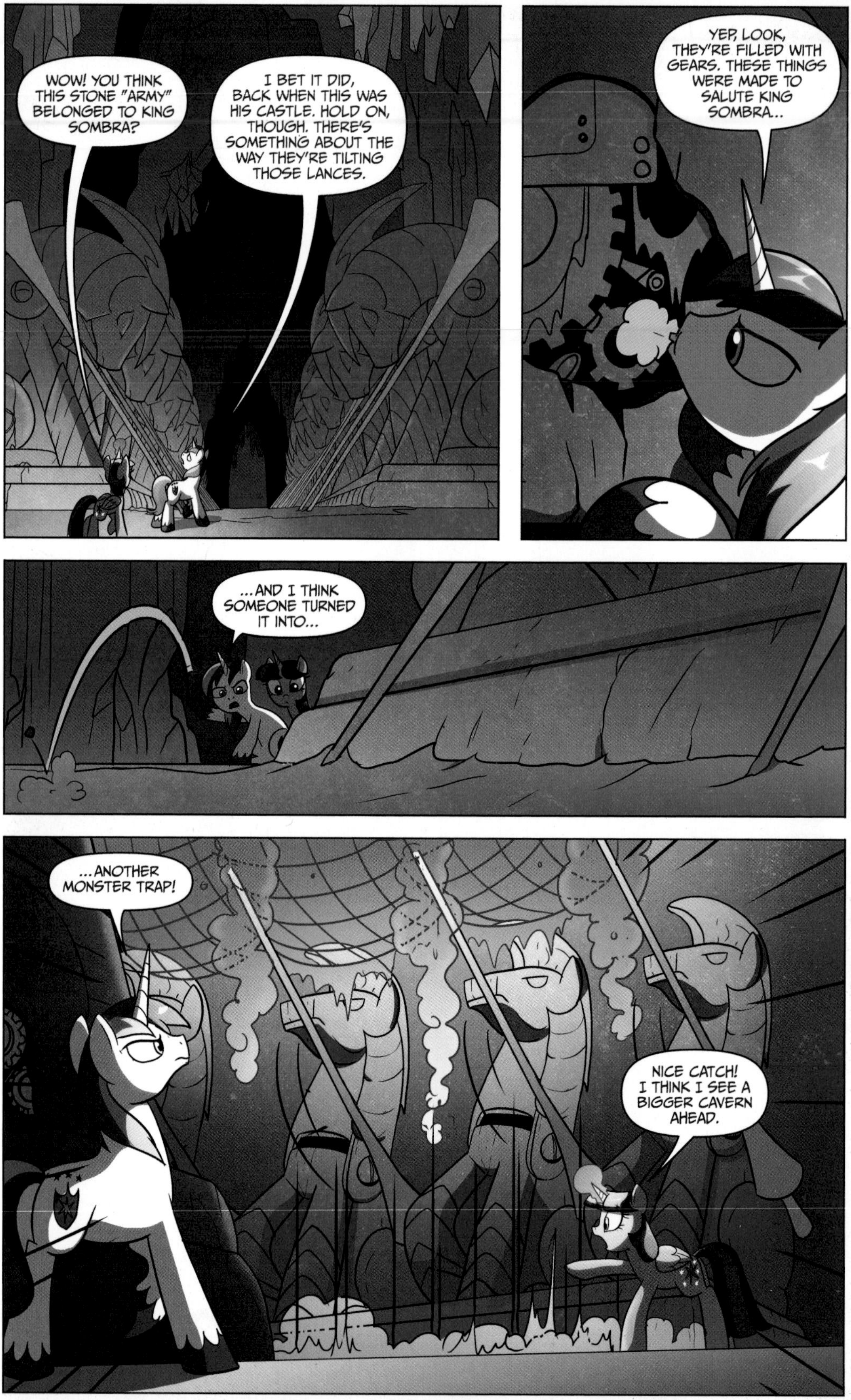
WOW! YOU THINK THIS STONE "ARMY" BELONGED TO KING SOMBRA?
I BET IT DID, BACK WHEN THIS WAS HIS CASTLE. HOLD ON, THOUGH. THERE'S SOMETHING ABOUT THE WAY THEY'RE TILTING THOSE LANCES.
YEP, LOOK, THEY'RE FILLED WITH GEARS. THESE THINGS WERE MADE TO SALUTE KING SOMBRA...
...AND I THINK SOMEONE TURNED IT INTO...
...ANOTHER MONSTER TRAP!
NICE CATCH! I THINK I SEE A BIGGER CAVERN AHEAD.

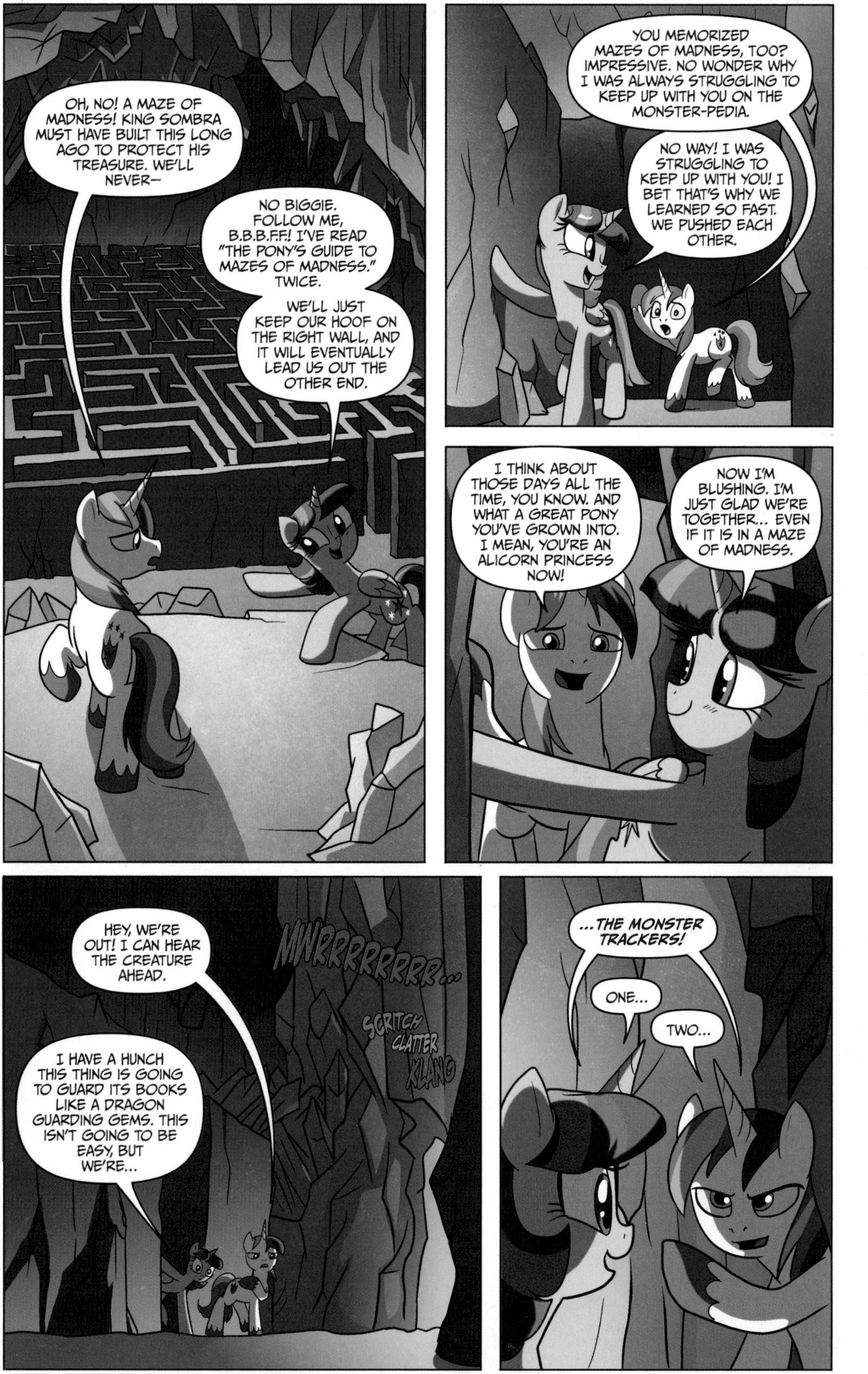
OH, NO! A MAZE OF MADNESS! KING SOMBRA MUST HAVE BUILT THIS LONG AGO TO PROTECT HIS TREASURE. WE'LL NEVER—
NO BIGGIE. FOLLOW ME, B.B.B.F.F.! I'VE READ "THE PONY'S GUIDE TO MAZES OF MADNESS." TWICE.
WE'LL JUST KEEP OUR HOOF ON THE RIGHT WALL, AND IT WILL EVENTUALLY LEAD US OUT THE OTHER END.
YOU MEMORIZED MAZES OF MADNESS, TOO? IMPRESSIVE. NO WONDER WHY I WAS ALWAYS STRUGGLING TO KEEP UP WITH YOU ON THE MONSTER-PEDIA.
NO WAY! I WAS STRUGGLING TO KEEP UP WITH YOU! I BET THAT'S WHY WE LEARNED SO FAST. WE PUSHED EACH OTHER.
I THINK ABOUT THOSE DAYS ALL THE TIME, YOU KNOW. AND WHAT A GREAT PONY YOU'VE GROWN INTO. I MEAN, YOU'RE AN ALICORN PRINCESS NOW!
NOW I'M BLUSHING. I'M JUST GLAD WE'RE TOGETHER... EVEN IF IT IS IN A MAZE OF MADNESS.
HEY, WE'RE OUT! I CAN HEAR THE CREATURE AHEAD.
MWRRRRRRRRR...
SCRITCH
CLATTER
KLANG
I HAVE A HUNCH THIS THING IS GOING TO GUARD ITS BOOKS LIKE A DRAGON GUARDING GEMS. THIS ISN'T GOING TO BE EASY, BUT WE'RE...
ONE...
TWO...
...THE MONSTER TRACKERS!

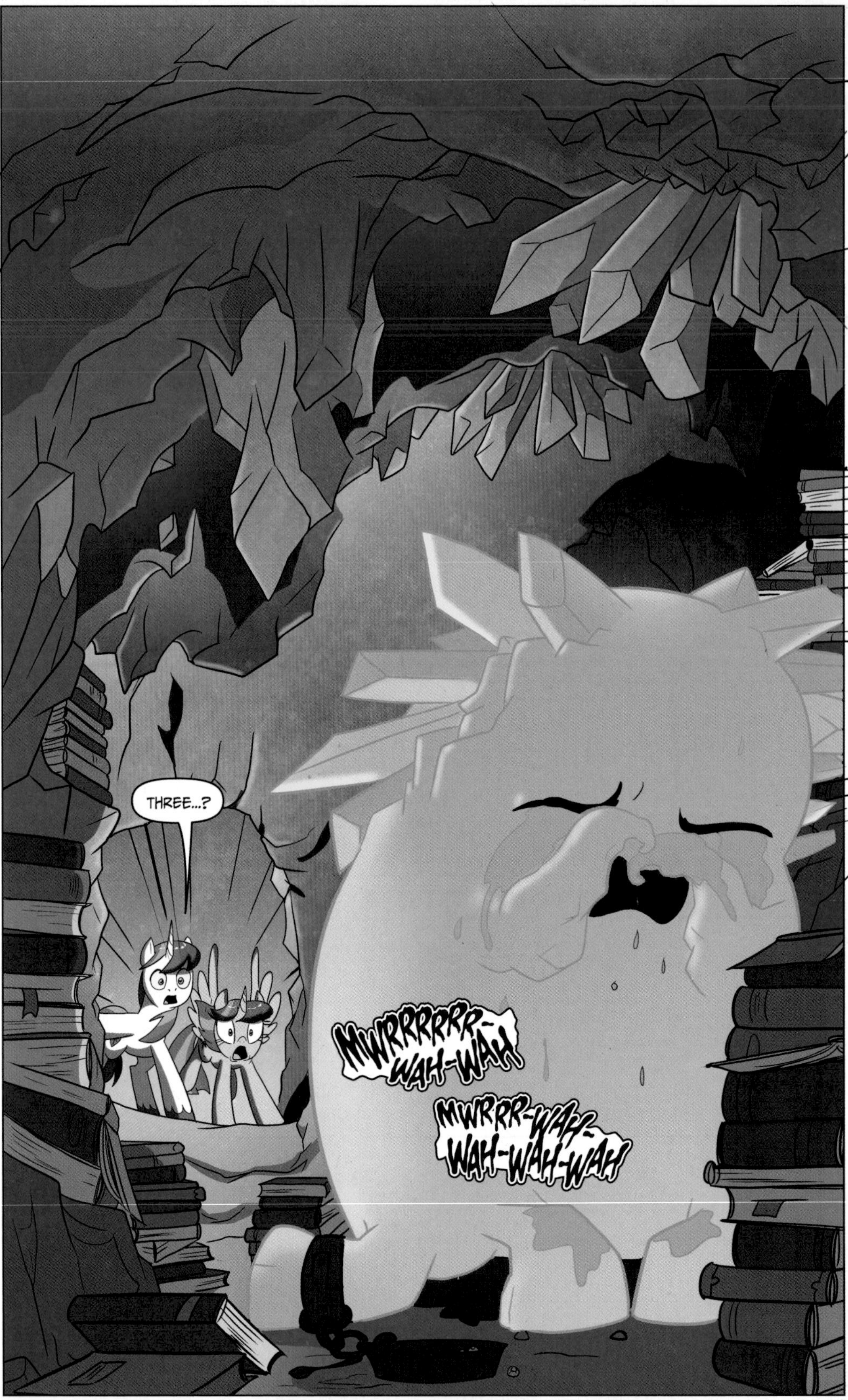
THREE...?
MWRRRRRR-WAH-WAH
MWRRR-WAH-WAH-WAH-WAH

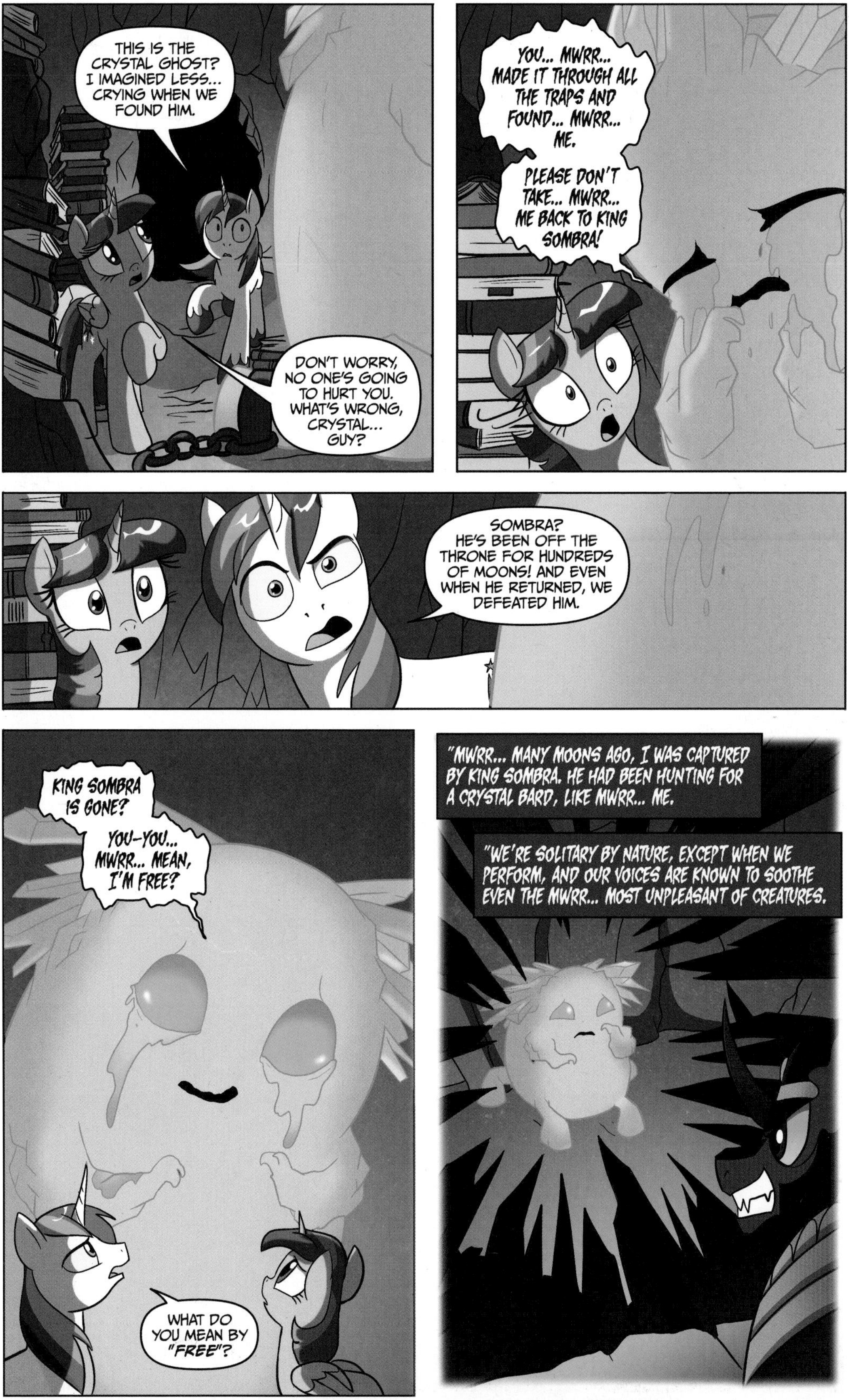
THIS IS THE CRYSTAL GHOST? I IMAGINED LESS... CRYING WHEN WE FOUND HIM.
DON'T WORRY, NO ONE'S GOING TO HURT YOU. WHAT'S WRONG, CRYSTAL... GUY?
YOU... MWRR... MADE IT THROUGH ALL THE TRAPS AND FOUND... MWRR... ME.
PLEASE DON'T TAKE... MWRR... ME BACK TO KING SOMBRA!
SOMBRA? HE'S BEEN OFF THE THRONE FOR HUNDREDS OF MOONS! AND EVEN WHEN HE RETURNED, WE DEFEATED HIM.
KING SOMBRA IS GONE?
YOU-YOU... MWRR... MEAN, I'M FREE?
WHAT DO YOU MEAN BY "FREE"?
"MWRR... MANY MOONS AGO, I WAS CAPTURED BY KING SOMBRA. HE HAD BEEN HUNTING FOR A CRYSTAL BARD, LIKE MWRR... ME.
"WE'RE SOLITARY BY NATURE, EXCEPT WHEN WE PERFORM, AND OUR VOICES ARE KNOWN TO SOOTHE EVEN THE MWRR... MOST UNPLEASANT OF CREATURES.

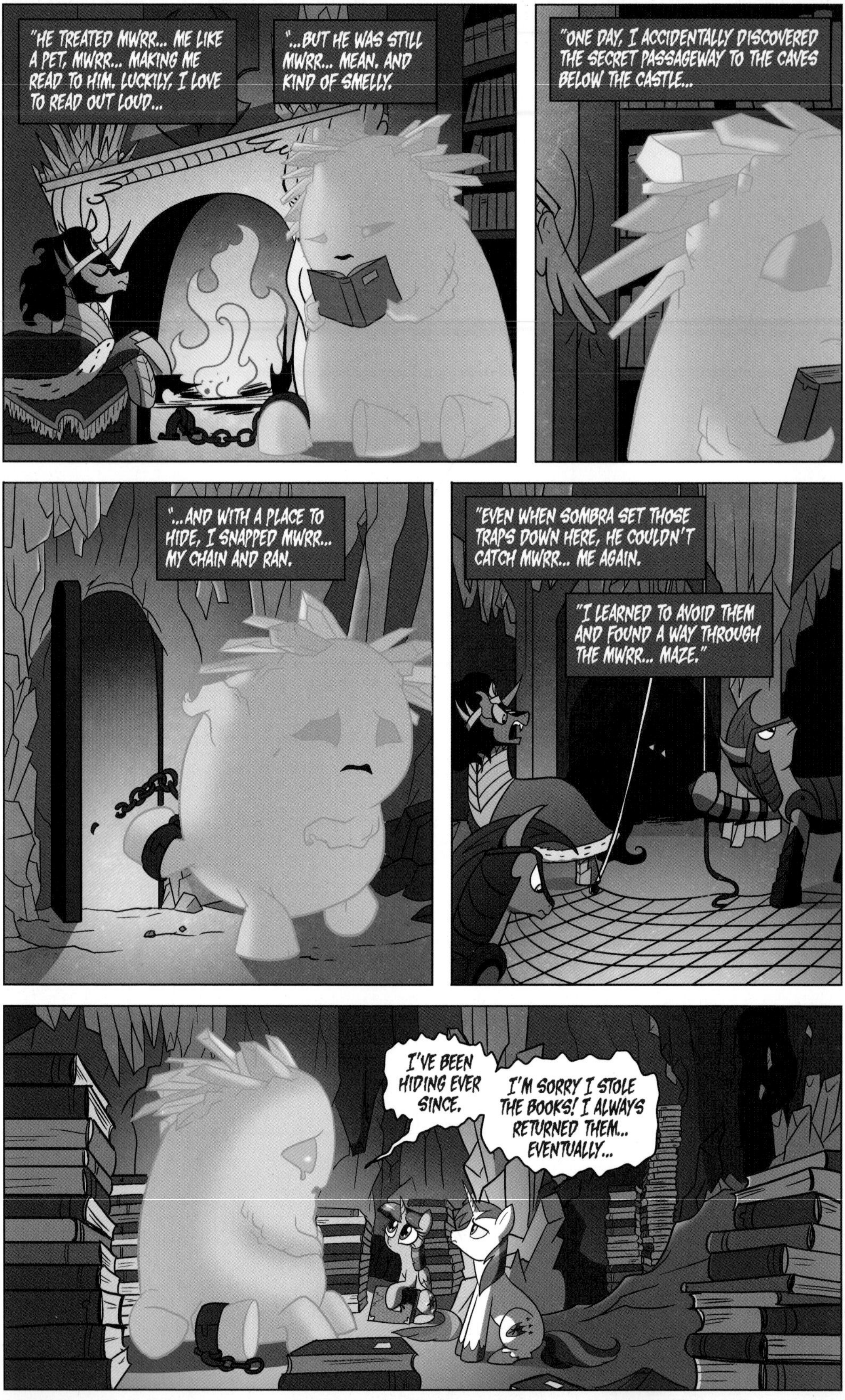
"HE TREATED MWRR... ME LIKE A PET, MWRR... MAKING ME READ TO HIM. LUCKILY, I LOVE TO READ OUT LOUD...
"...BUT HE WAS STILL MWRR... MEAN. AND KIND OF SMELLY.
"ONE DAY, I ACCIDENTALLY DISCOVERED THE SECRET PASSAGEWAY TO THE CAVES BELOW THE CASTLE...
"...AND WITH A PLACE TO HIDE, I SNAPPED MWRR... MY CHAIN AND RAN.
"EVEN WHEN SOMBRA SET THOSE TRAPS DOWN HERE, HE COULDN'T CATCH MWRR... ME AGAIN.
"I LEARNED TO AVOID THEM AND FOUND A WAY THROUGH THE MWRR... MAZE."
I'VE BEEN HIDING EVER SINCE.
I'M SORRY I STOLE THE BOOKS! I ALWAYS RETURNED THEM... EVENTUALLY...

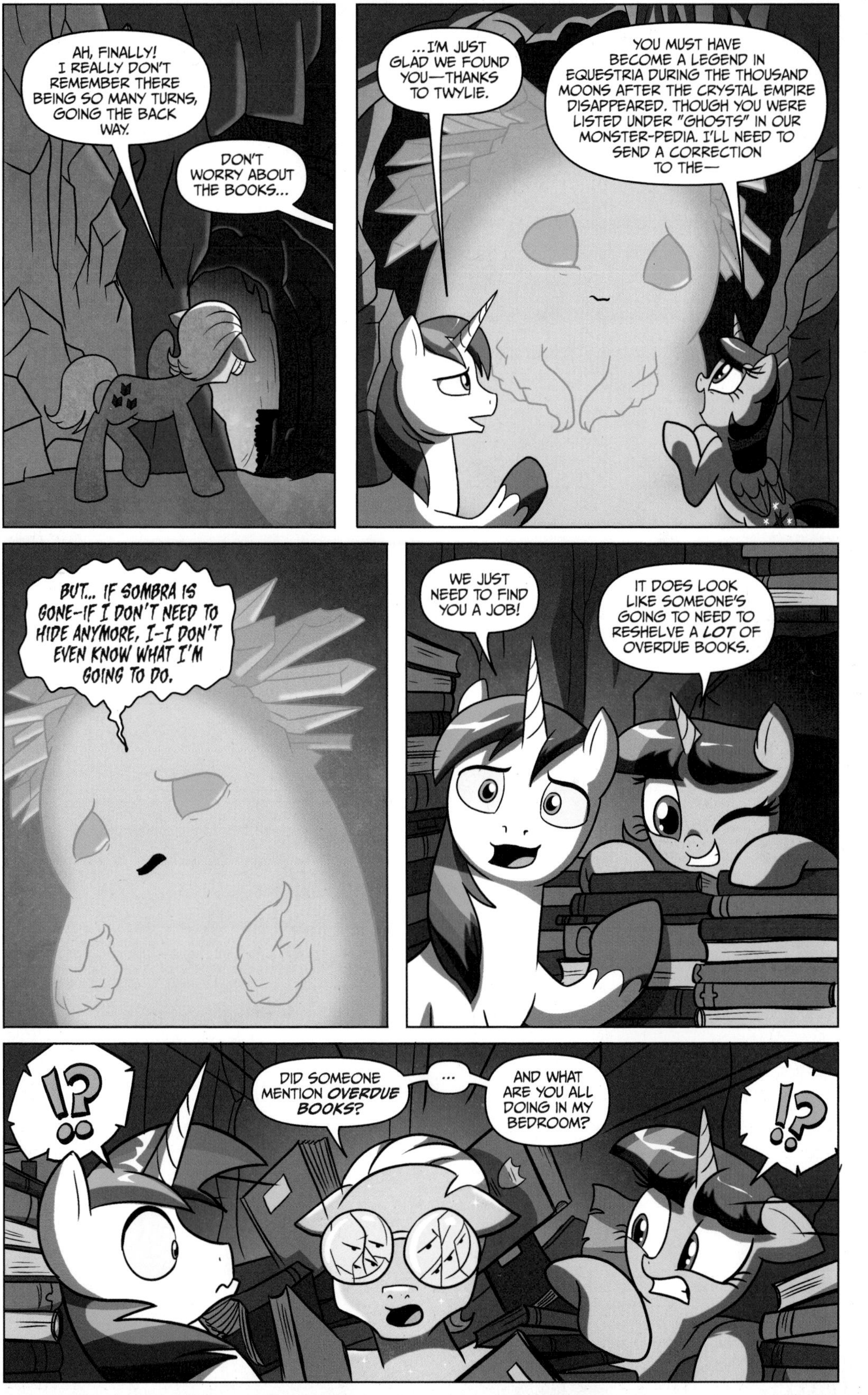
AH, FINALLY! I REALLY DON'T REMEMBER THERE BEING SO MANY TURNS, GOING THE BACK WAY.
DON'T WORRY ABOUT THE BOOKS...
...I'M JUST GLAD WE FOUND YOU—THANKS TO TWYLIE.
YOU MUST HAVE BECOME A LEGEND IN EQUESTRIA DURING THE THOUSAND MOONS AFTER THE CRYSTAL EMPIRE DISAPPEARED. THOUGH YOU WERE LISTED UNDER "GHOSTS" IN OUR MONSTER-PEDIA. I'LL NEED TO SEND A CORRECTION TO THE—
BUT... IF SOMBRA IS GONE—IF I DON'T NEED TO HIDE ANYMORE, I—I DON'T EVEN KNOW WHAT I'M GOING TO DO.
WE JUST NEED TO FIND YOU A JOB!
IT DOES LOOK LIKE SOMEONE'S GOING TO NEED TO RESHELVE A *LOT* OF OVERDUE BOOKS.
!?
DID SOMEONE MENTION *OVERDUE BOOKS*?
...
AND WHAT ARE YOU ALL DOING IN MY BEDROOM?
!?

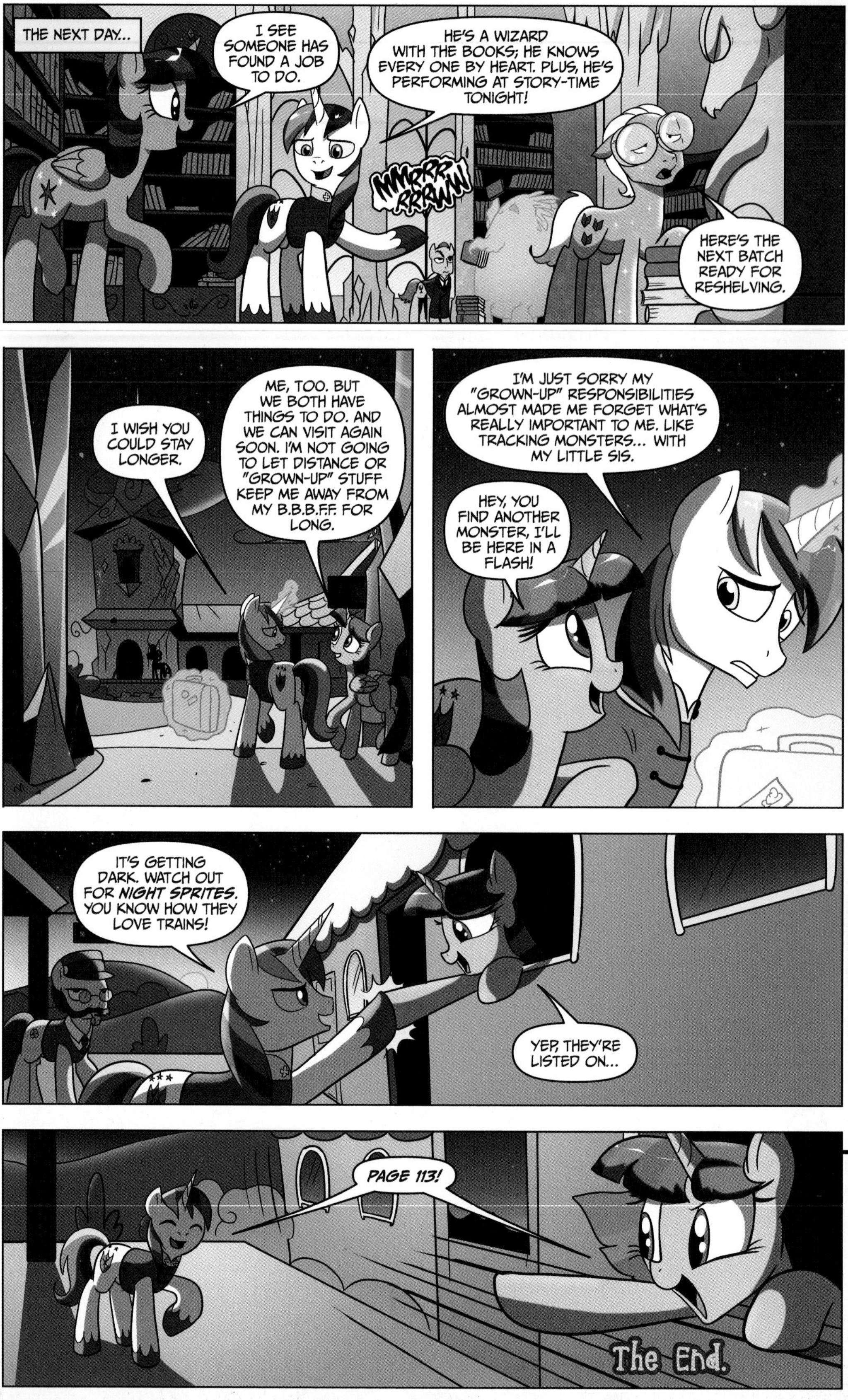
THE NEXT DAY...
I SEE SOMEONE HAS FOUND A JOB TO DO.
HE'S A WIZARD WITH THE BOOKS; HE KNOWS EVERY ONE BY HEART. PLUS, HE'S PERFORMING AT STORY-TIME TONIGHT!
MMRRR RRRAWW
HERE'S THE NEXT BATCH READY FOR RESHELVING.
I WISH YOU COULD STAY LONGER.
ME, TOO. BUT WE BOTH HAVE THINGS TO DO. AND WE CAN VISIT AGAIN SOON. I'M NOT GOING TO LET DISTANCE OR "GROWN-UP" STUFF KEEP ME AWAY FROM MY B.B.B.F.F. FOR LONG.
I'M JUST SORRY MY "GROWN-UP" RESPONSIBILITIES ALMOST MADE ME FORGET WHAT'S REALLY IMPORTANT TO ME. LIKE TRACKING MONSTERS... WITH MY LITTLE SIS.
HEY, YOU FIND ANOTHER MONSTER, I'LL BE HERE IN A FLASH!
IT'S GETTING DARK. WATCH OUT FOR *NIGHT SPRITES*. YOU KNOW HOW THEY LOVE TRAINS!
YEP, THEY'RE LISTED ON...
PAGE 113!
The End.

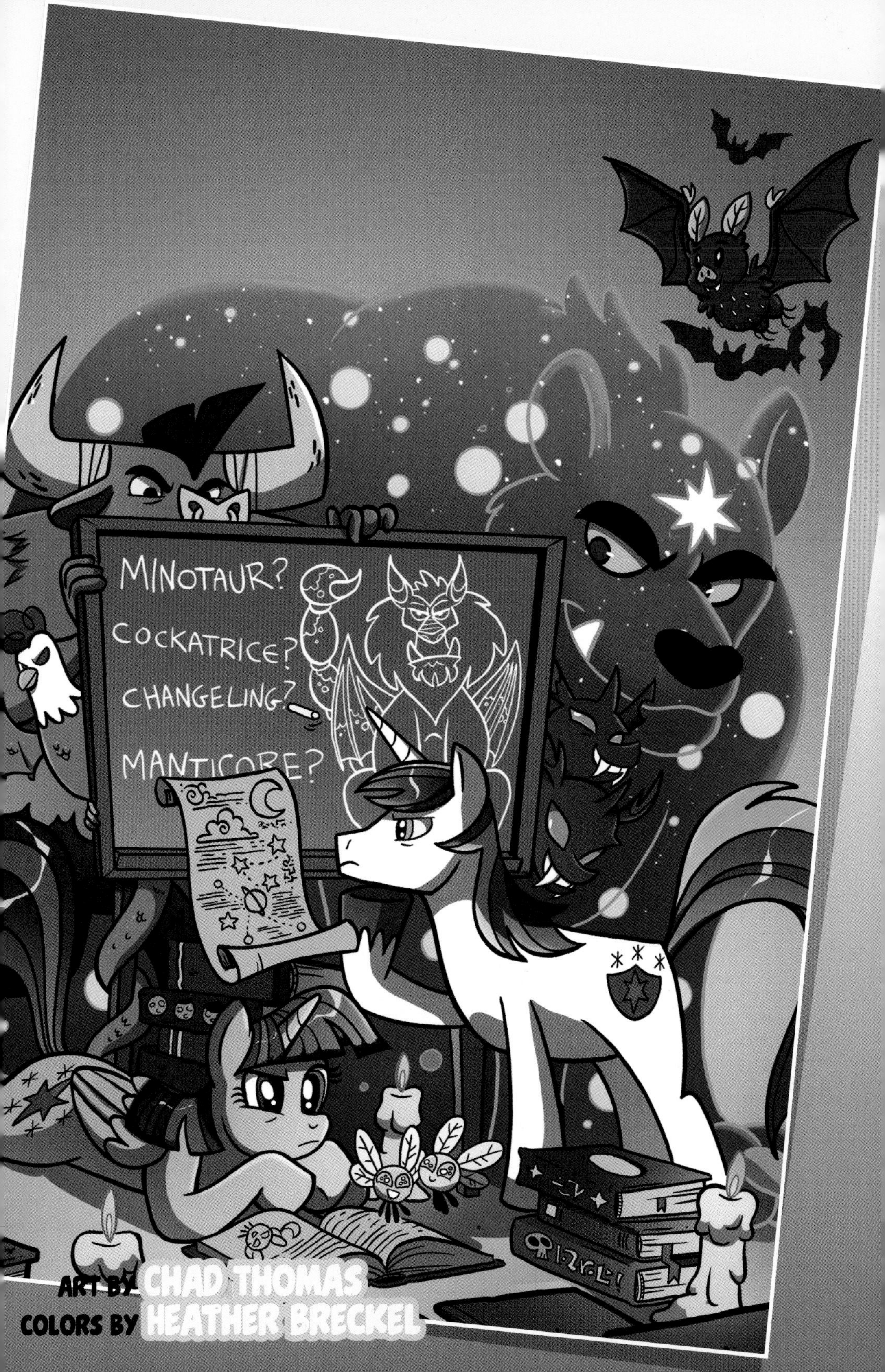
MINOTAUR?
COCKATRICE?
CHANGELING?
MANTICORE?

ART BY CHAD THOMAS
COLORS BY HEATHER BRECKEL

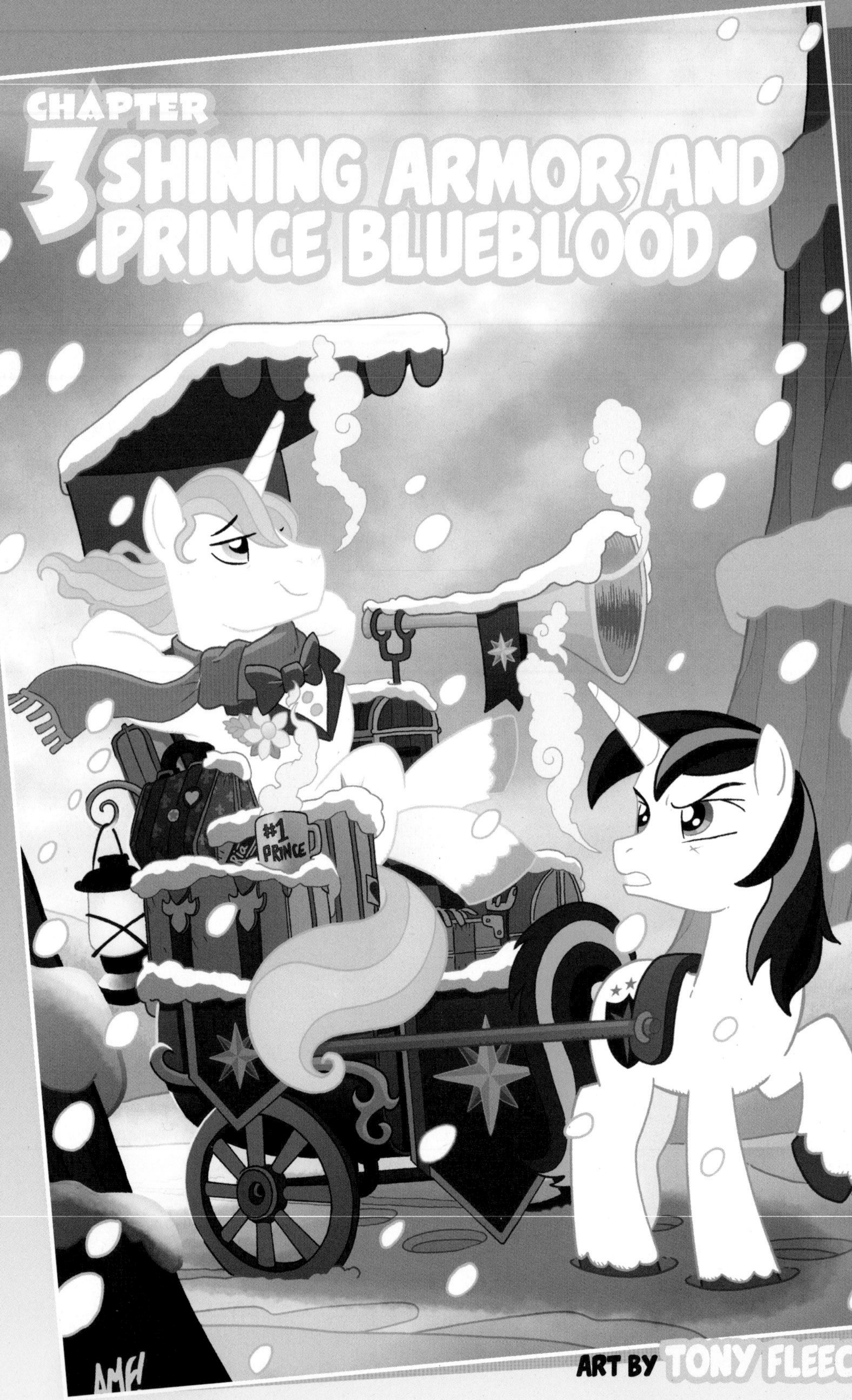
CHAPTER 3
SHINING ARMOR AND PRINCE BLUEBLOOD
#1 PRINCE

ART BY TONY FLEECS

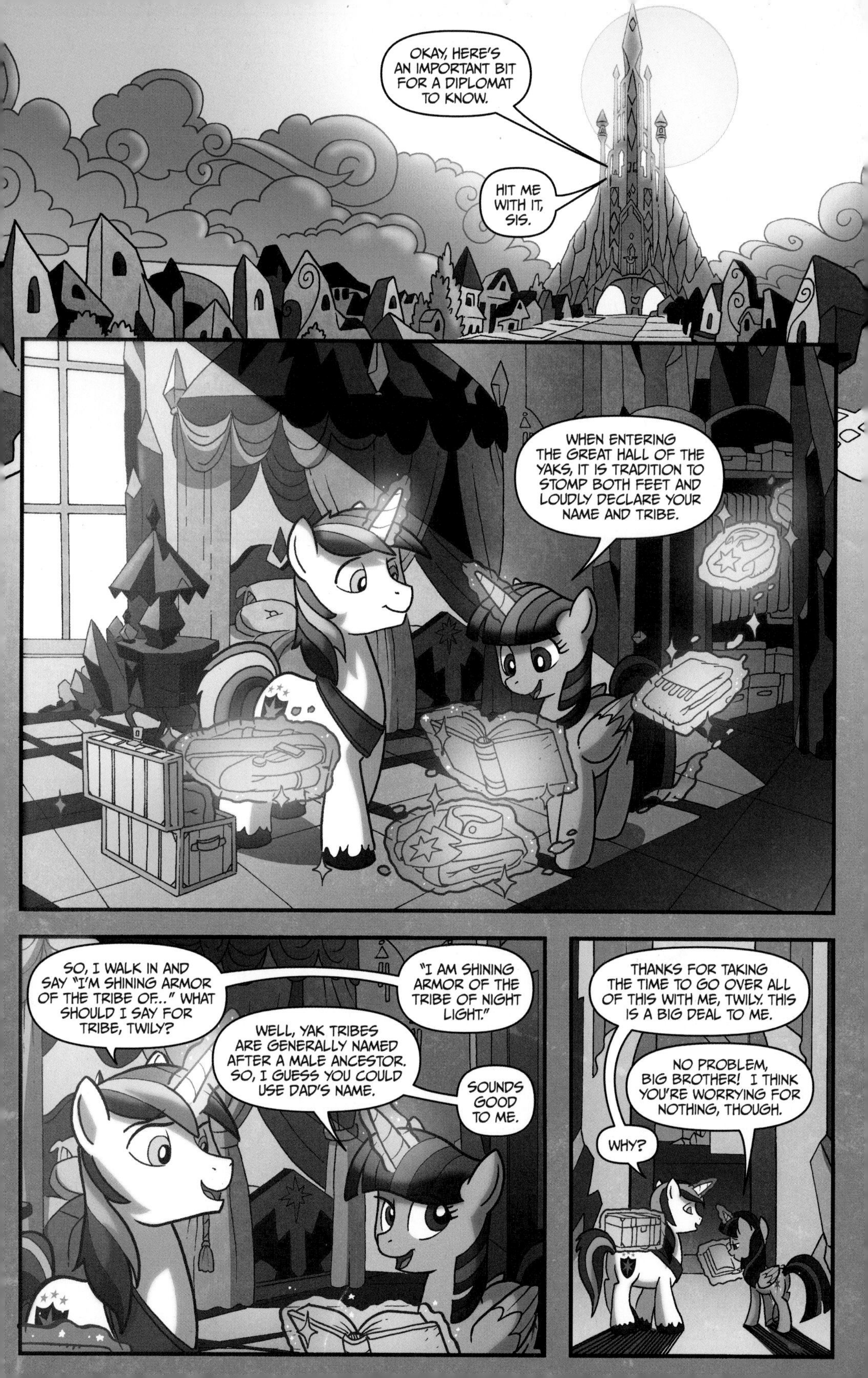
OKAY, HERE'S AN IMPORTANT BIT FOR A DIPLOMAT TO KNOW.
HIT ME WITH IT, SIS.
WHEN ENTERING THE GREAT HALL OF THE YAKS, IT IS TRADITION TO STOMP BOTH FEET AND LOUDLY DECLARE YOUR NAME AND TRIBE.
SO, I WALK IN AND SAY "I'M SHINING ARMOR OF THE TRIBE OF..." WHAT SHOULD I SAY FOR TRIBE, TWILY?
WELL, YAK TRIBES ARE GENERALLY NAMED AFTER A MALE ANCESTOR. SO, I GUESS YOU COULD USE DAD'S NAME.
"I AM SHINING ARMOR OF THE TRIBE OF NIGHT LIGHT."
SOUNDS GOOD TO ME.
THANKS FOR TAKING THE TIME TO GO OVER ALL OF THIS WITH ME, TWILY. THIS IS A BIG DEAL TO ME.
NO PROBLEM, BIG BROTHER! I THINK YOU'RE WORRYING FOR NOTHING, THOUGH.
WHY?

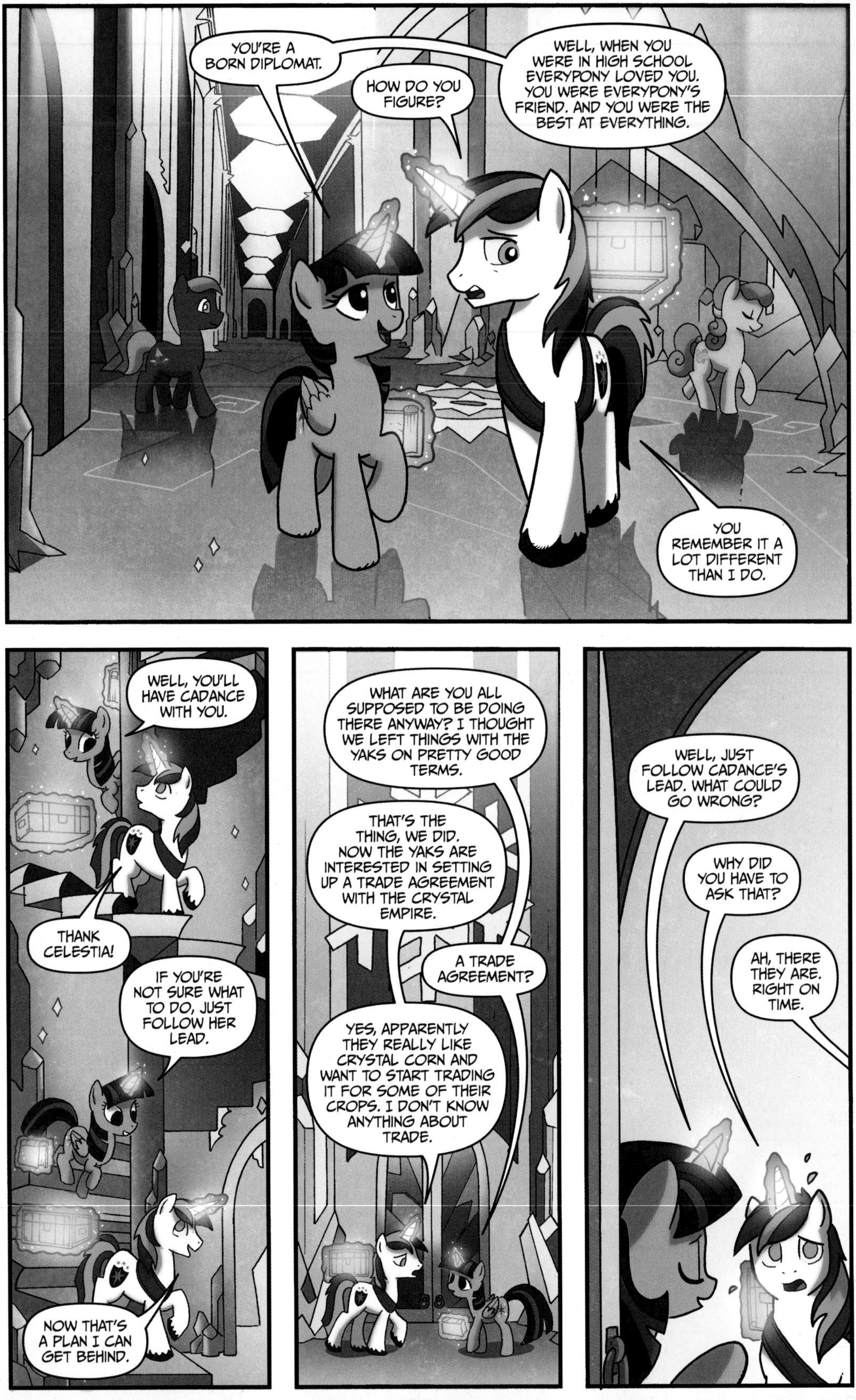
YOU'RE A BORN DIPLOMAT.
HOW DO YOU FIGURE?
WELL, WHEN YOU WERE IN HIGH SCHOOL EVERYPONY LOVED YOU. YOU WERE EVERYPONY'S FRIEND. AND YOU WERE THE BEST AT EVERYTHING.
YOU REMEMBER IT A LOT DIFFERENT THAN I DO.
WELL, YOU'LL HAVE CADANCE WITH YOU.
THANK CELESTIA!
IF YOU'RE NOT SURE WHAT TO DO, JUST FOLLOW HER LEAD.
NOW THAT'S A PLAN I CAN GET BEHIND.
WHAT ARE YOU ALL SUPPOSED TO BE DOING THERE ANYWAY? I THOUGHT WE LEFT THINGS WITH THE YAKS ON PRETTY GOOD TERMS.
THAT'S THE THING, WE DID. NOW THE YAKS ARE INTERESTED IN SETTING UP A TRADE AGREEMENT WITH THE CRYSTAL EMPIRE.
A TRADE AGREEMENT?
YES, APPARENTLY THEY REALLY LIKE CRYSTAL CORN AND WANT TO START TRADING IT FOR SOME OF THEIR CROPS. I DON'T KNOW ANYTHING ABOUT TRADE.
WELL, JUST FOLLOW CADANCE'S LEAD. WHAT COULD GO WRONG?
WHY DID YOU HAVE TO ASK THAT?
AH, THERE THEY ARE. RIGHT ON TIME.

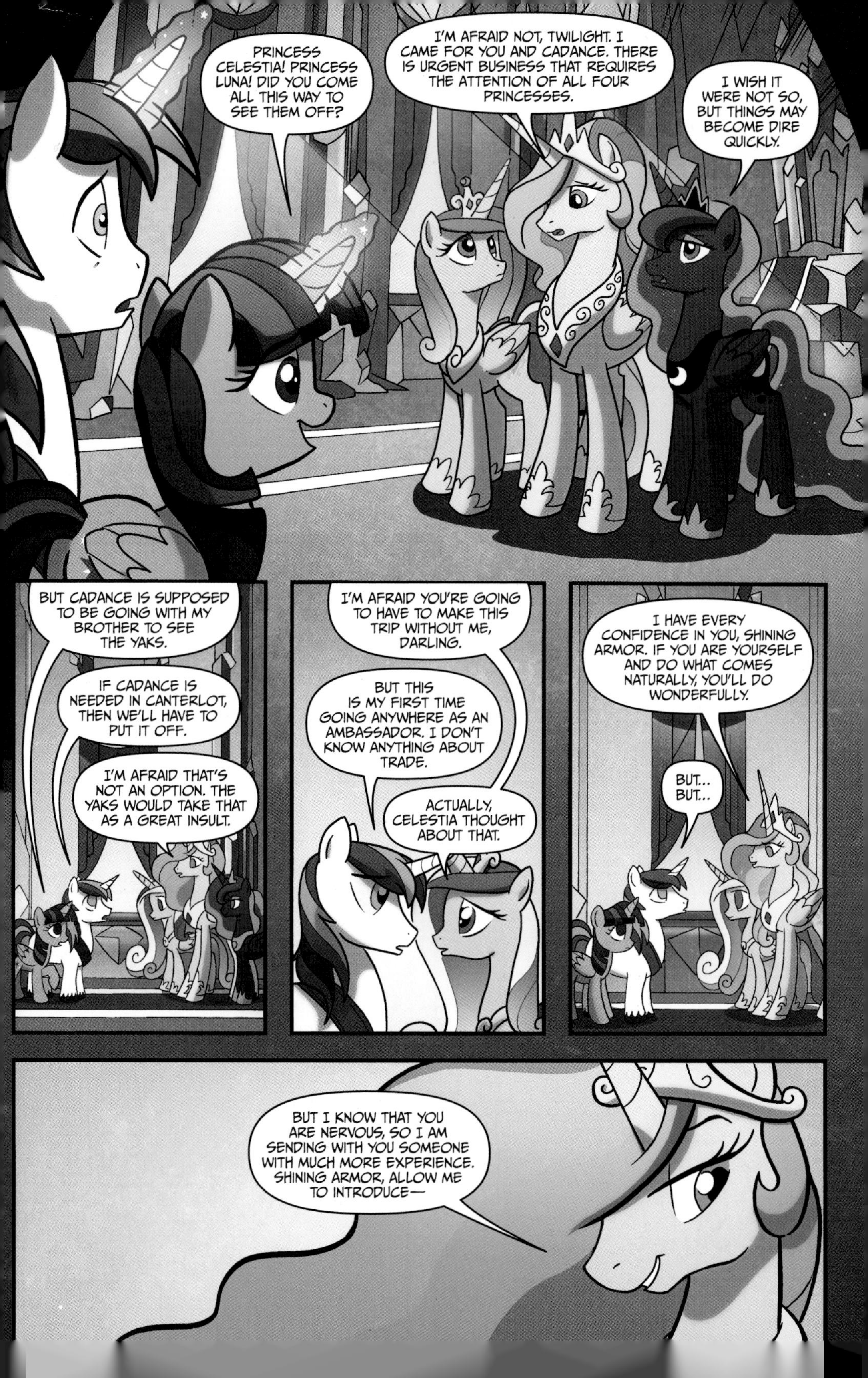

PRINCESS CELESTIA! PRINCESS LUNA! DID YOU COME ALL THIS WAY TO SEE THEM OFF?
I'M AFRAID NOT, TWILIGHT. I CAME FOR YOU AND CADANCE. THERE IS URGENT BUSINESS THAT REQUIRES THE ATTENTION OF ALL FOUR PRINCESSES.
I WISH IT WERE NOT SO, BUT THINGS MAY BECOME DIRE QUICKLY.
BUT CADANCE IS SUPPOSED TO BE GOING WITH MY BROTHER TO SEE THE YAKS.
IF CADANCE IS NEEDED IN CANTERLOT, THEN WE'LL HAVE TO PUT IT OFF.
I'M AFRAID THAT'S NOT AN OPTION. THE YAKS WOULD TAKE THAT AS A GREAT INSULT.
I'M AFRAID YOU'RE GOING TO HAVE TO MAKE THIS TRIP WITHOUT ME, DARLING.
BUT THIS IS MY FIRST TIME GOING ANYWHERE AS AN AMBASSADOR. I DON'T KNOW ANYTHING ABOUT TRADE.
ACTUALLY, CELESTIA THOUGHT ABOUT THAT.
I HAVE EVERY CONFIDENCE IN YOU, SHINING ARMOR. IF YOU ARE YOURSELF AND DO WHAT COMES NATURALLY, YOU'LL DO WONDERFULLY.
BUT... BUT...
BUT I KNOW THAT YOU ARE NERVOUS, SO I AM SENDING WITH YOU SOMEONE WITH MUCH MORE EXPERIENCE. SHINING ARMOR, ALLOW ME TO INTRODUCE—

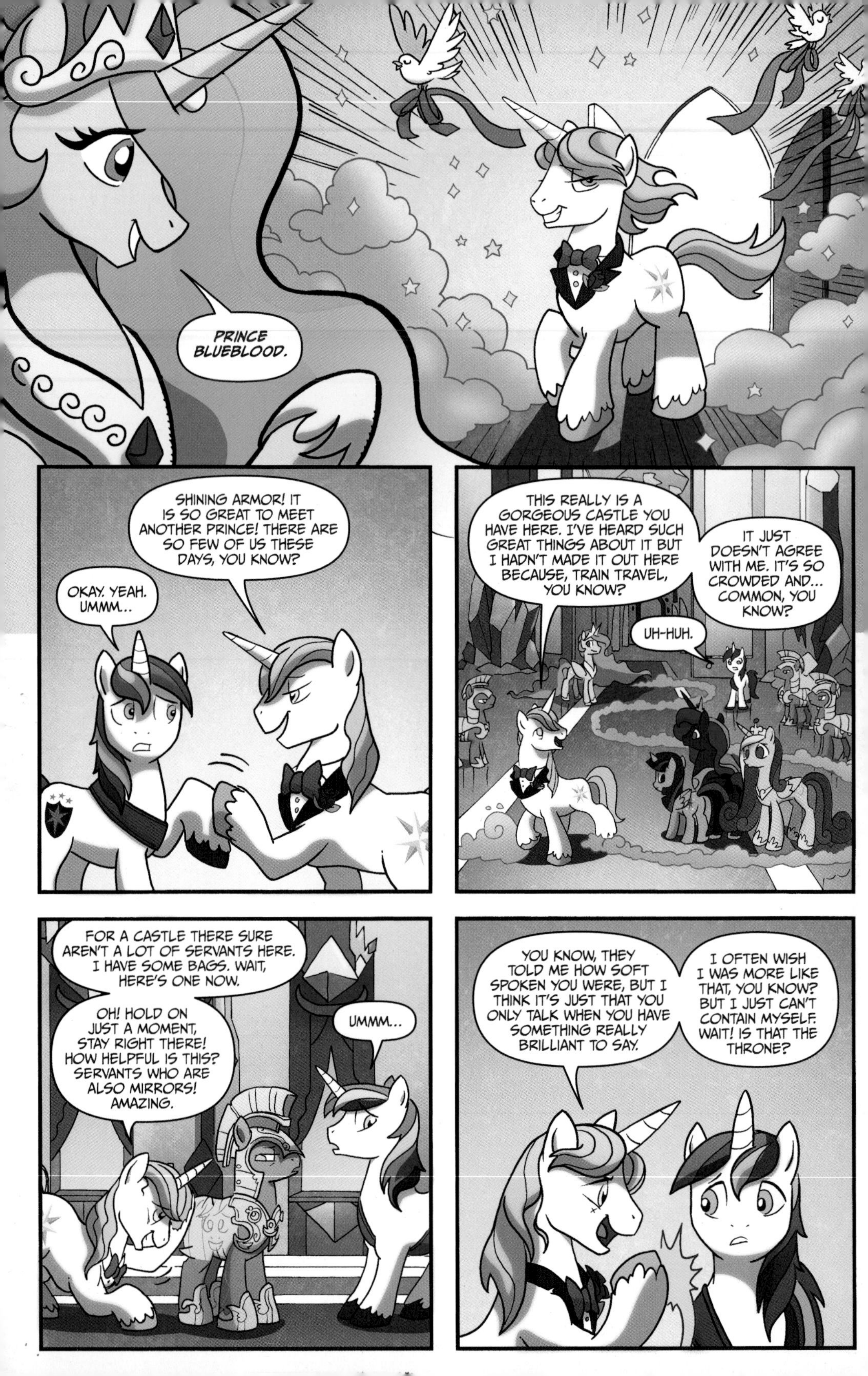
PRINCE BLUEBLOOD.
SHINING ARMOR! IT IS SO GREAT TO MEET ANOTHER PRINCE! THERE ARE SO FEW OF US THESE DAYS, YOU KNOW?
OKAY. YEAH. UMMM...
THIS REALLY IS A GORGEOUS CASTLE YOU HAVE HERE. I'VE HEARD SUCH GREAT THINGS ABOUT IT BUT I HADN'T MADE IT OUT HERE BECAUSE, TRAIN TRAVEL, YOU KNOW?
IT JUST DOESN'T AGREE WITH ME. IT'S SO CROWDED AND... COMMON, YOU KNOW?
UH-HUH.
FOR A CASTLE THERE SURE AREN'T A LOT OF SERVANTS HERE. I HAVE SOME BAGS. WAIT, HERE'S ONE NOW.
OH! HOLD ON JUST A MOMENT, STAY RIGHT THERE! HOW HELPFUL IS THIS? SERVANTS WHO ARE ALSO MIRRORS! AMAZING.
UMMM...
YOU KNOW, THEY TOLD ME HOW SOFT SPOKEN YOU WERE, BUT I THINK IT'S JUST THAT YOU ONLY TALK WHEN YOU HAVE SOMETHING REALLY BRILLIANT TO SAY.
I OFTEN WISH I WAS MORE LIKE THAT, YOU KNOW? BUT I JUST CAN'T CONTAIN MYSELF. WAIT! IS THAT THE THRONE?

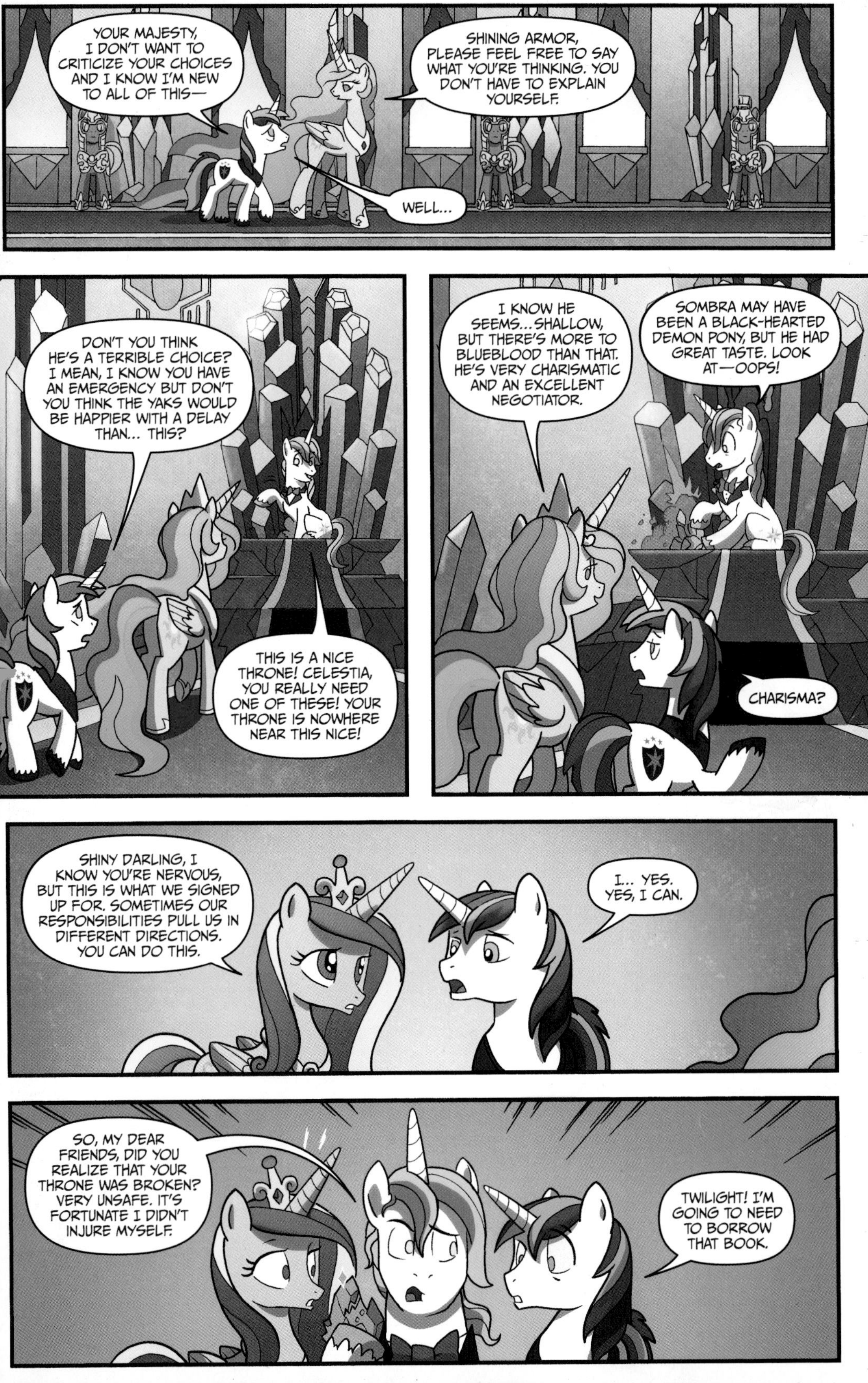
YOUR MAJESTY, I DON'T WANT TO CRITICIZE YOUR CHOICES AND I KNOW I'M NEW TO ALL OF THIS—
SHINING ARMOR, PLEASE FEEL FREE TO SAY WHAT YOU'RE THINKING. YOU DON'T HAVE TO EXPLAIN YOURSELF.
WELL...
DON'T YOU THINK HE'S A TERRIBLE CHOICE? I MEAN, I KNOW YOU HAVE AN EMERGENCY BUT DON'T YOU THINK THE YAKS WOULD BE HAPPIER WITH A DELAY THAN... THIS?
THIS IS A NICE THRONE! CELESTIA, YOU REALLY NEED ONE OF THESE! YOUR THRONE IS NOWHERE NEAR THIS NICE!
I KNOW HE SEEMS...SHALLOW, BUT THERE'S MORE TO BLUEBLOOD THAN THAT. HE'S VERY CHARISMATIC AND AN EXCELLENT NEGOTIATOR.
SOMBRA MAY HAVE BEEN A BLACK-HEARTED DEMON PONY, BUT HE HAD GREAT TASTE. LOOK AT—OOPS!
CHARISMA?
SHINY DARLING, I KNOW YOU'RE NERVOUS, BUT THIS IS WHAT WE SIGNED UP FOR. SOMETIMES OUR RESPONSIBILITIES PULL US IN DIFFERENT DIRECTIONS. YOU CAN DO THIS.
I... YES. YES, I CAN.
SO, MY DEAR FRIENDS, DID YOU REALIZE THAT YOUR THRONE WAS BROKEN? VERY UNSAFE. IT'S FORTUNATE I DIDN'T INJURE MYSELF.
TWILIGHT! I'M GOING TO NEED TO BORROW THAT BOOK.

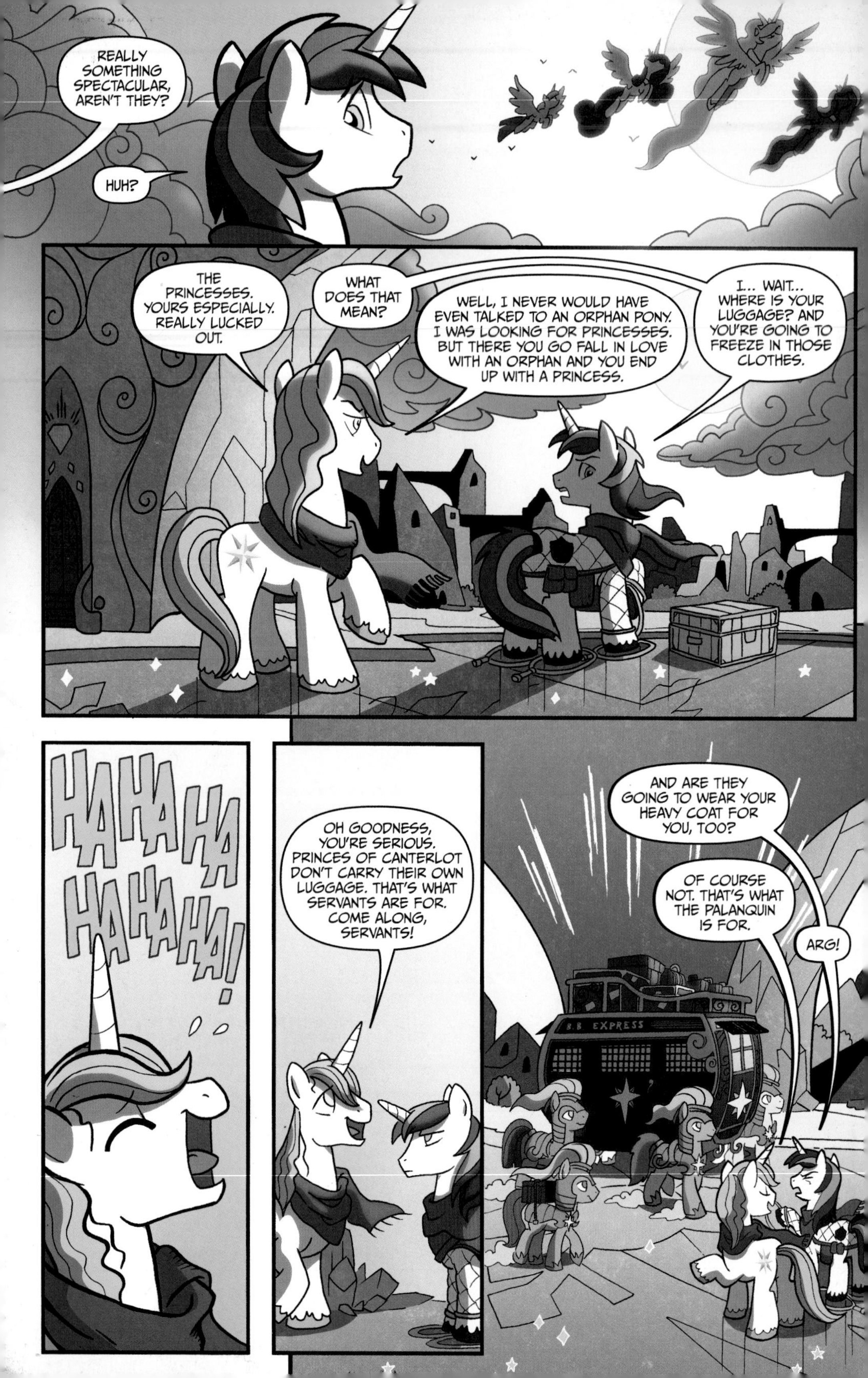
REALLY SOMETHING SPECTACULAR, AREN'T THEY?
HUH?
THE PRINCESSES. YOURS ESPECIALLY. REALLY LUCKED OUT.
WHAT DOES THAT MEAN?
WELL, I NEVER WOULD HAVE EVEN TALKED TO AN ORPHAN PONY. I WAS LOOKING FOR PRINCESSES. BUT THERE YOU GO FALL IN LOVE WITH AN ORPHAN AND YOU END UP WITH A PRINCESS.
I... WAIT... WHERE IS YOUR LUGGAGE? AND YOU'RE GOING TO FREEZE IN THOSE CLOTHES.
HAHAHA HAHAHA!
OH GOODNESS, YOU'RE SERIOUS. PRINCES OF CANTERLOT DON'T CARRY THEIR OWN LUGGAGE. THAT'S WHAT SERVANTS ARE FOR. COME ALONG, SERVANTS!
AND ARE THEY GOING TO WEAR YOUR HEAVY COAT FOR YOU, TOO?
OF COURSE NOT. THAT'S WHAT THE PALANQUIN IS FOR.
ARG!
B.B EXPRESS

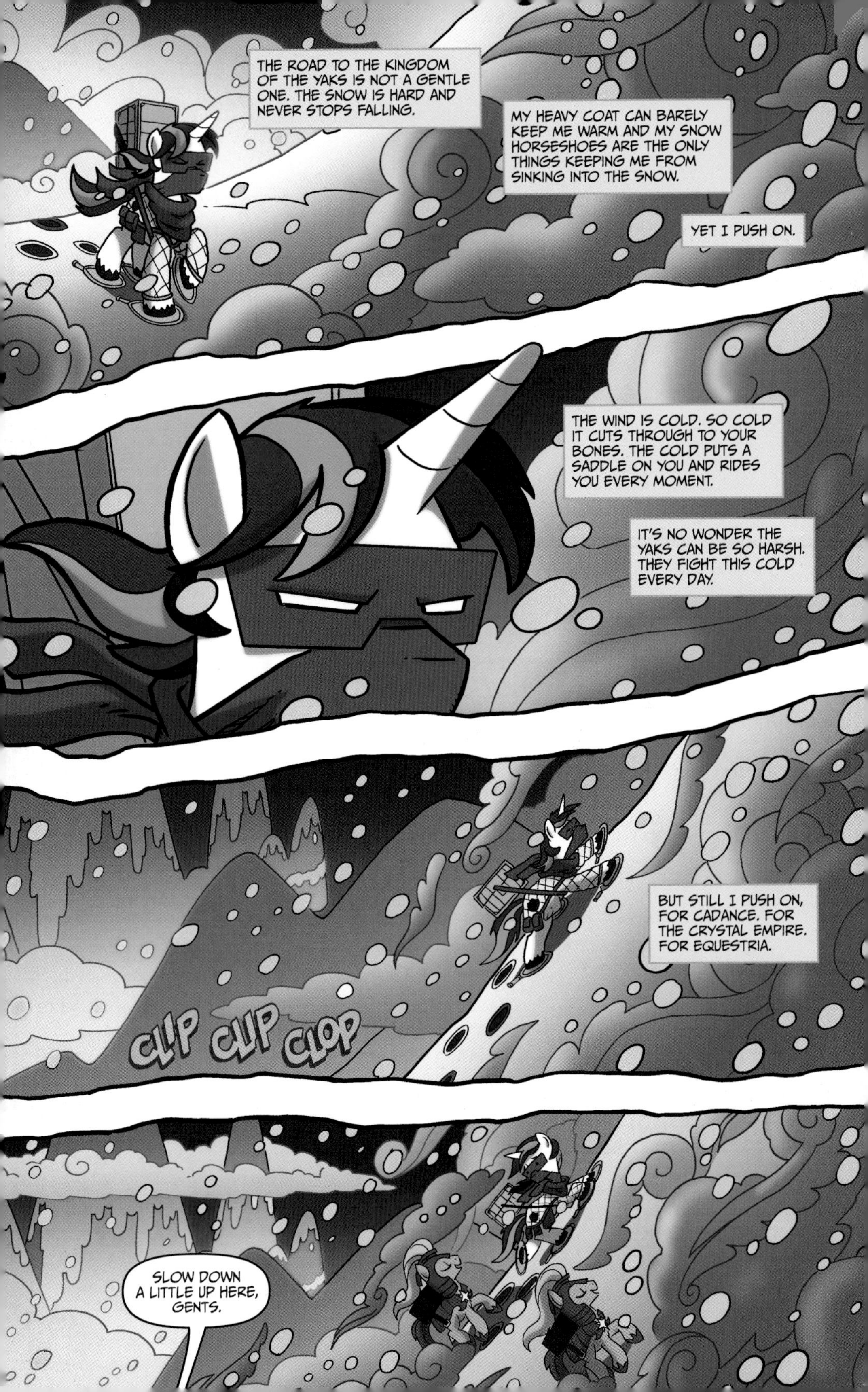
THE ROAD TO THE KINGDOM OF THE YAKS IS NOT A GENTLE ONE. THE SNOW IS HARD AND NEVER STOPS FALLING.
MY HEAVY COAT CAN BARELY KEEP ME WARM AND MY SNOW HORSESHOES ARE THE ONLY THINGS KEEPING ME FROM SINKING INTO THE SNOW.
YET I PUSH ON.
THE WIND IS COLD. SO COLD IT CUTS THROUGH TO YOUR BONES. THE COLD PUTS A SADDLE ON YOU AND RIDES YOU EVERY MOMENT.
IT'S NO WONDER THE YAKS CAN BE SO HARSH. THEY FIGHT THIS COLD EVERY DAY.
BUT STILL I PUSH ON, FOR CADANCE. FOR THE CRYSTAL EMPIRE. FOR EQUESTRIA.
CLIP CLIP CLOP
SLOW DOWN A LITTLE UP HERE, GENTS.

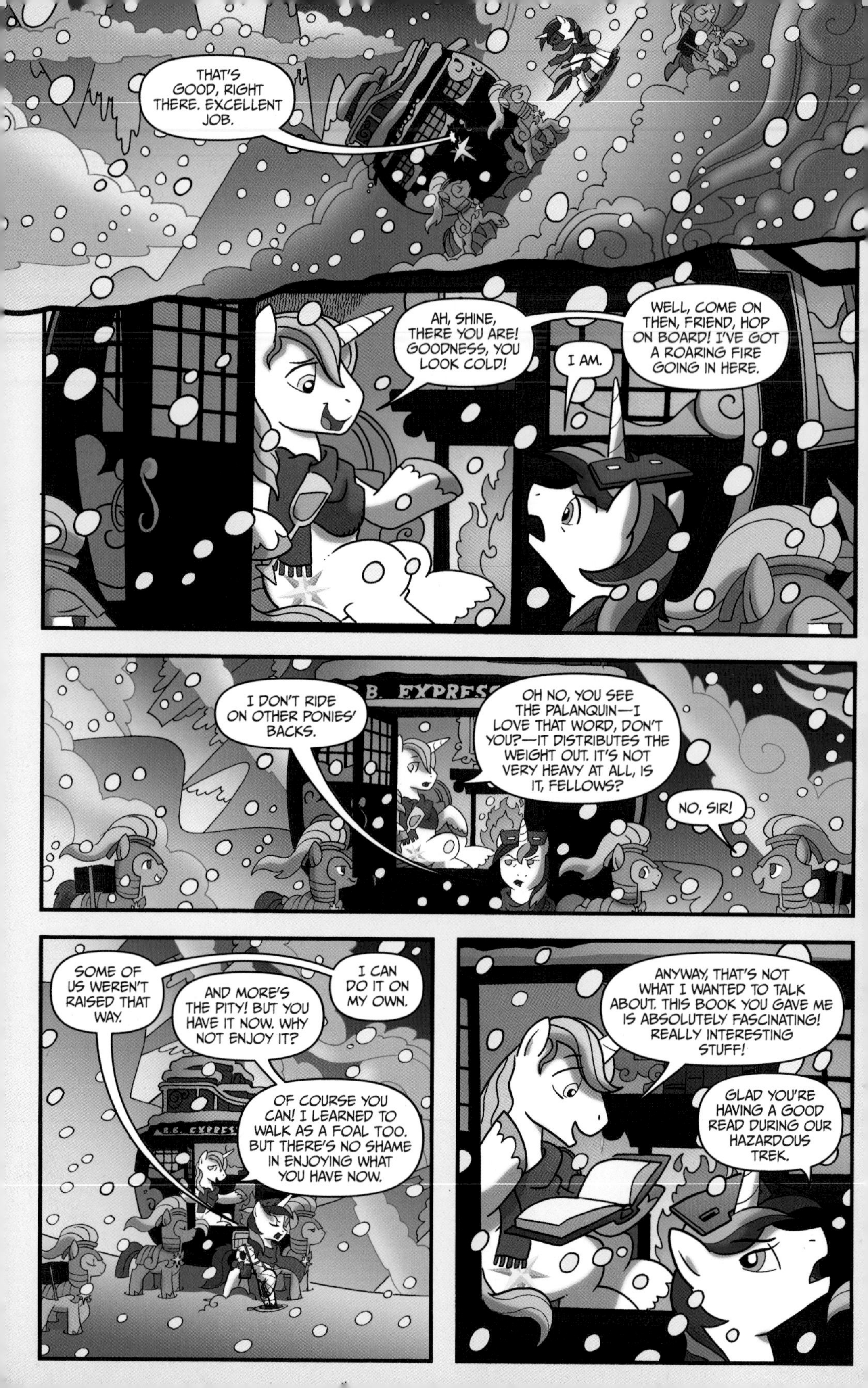
THAT'S GOOD, RIGHT THERE. EXCELLENT JOB.
AH, SHINE, THERE YOU ARE! GOODNESS, YOU LOOK COLD!
I AM.
WELL, COME ON THEN, FRIEND, HOP ON BOARD! I'VE GOT A ROARING FIRE GOING IN HERE.
B.B. EXPRESS
I DON'T RIDE ON OTHER PONIES' BACKS.
OH NO, YOU SEE THE PALANQUIN—I LOVE THAT WORD, DON'T YOU?—IT DISTRIBUTES THE WEIGHT OUT. IT'S NOT VERY HEAVY AT ALL, IS IT, FELLOWS?
NO, SIR!
SOME OF US WEREN'T RAISED THAT WAY.
AND MORE'S THE PITY! BUT YOU HAVE IT NOW. WHY NOT ENJOY IT?
I CAN DO IT ON MY OWN.
OF COURSE YOU CAN! I LEARNED TO WALK AS A FOAL TOO. BUT THERE'S NO SHAME IN ENJOYING WHAT YOU HAVE NOW.
ANYWAY, THAT'S NOT WHAT I WANTED TO TALK ABOUT. THIS BOOK YOU GAVE ME IS ABSOLUTELY FASCINATING! REALLY INTERESTING STUFF!
GLAD YOU'RE HAVING A GOOD READ DURING OUR HAZARDOUS TREK.

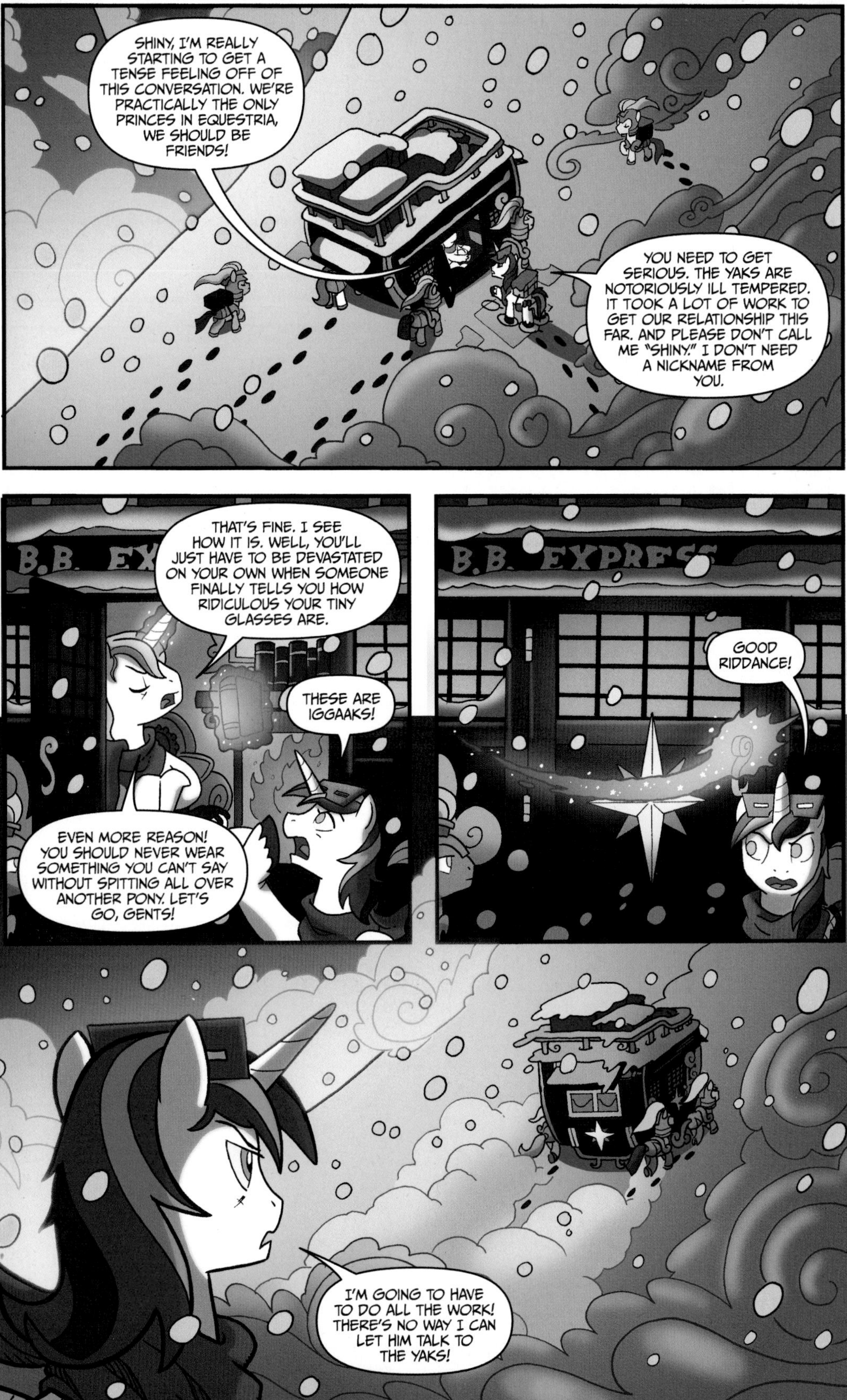
SHINY, I'M REALLY STARTING TO GET A TENSE FEELING OFF OF THIS CONVERSATION. WE'RE PRACTICALLY THE ONLY PRINCES IN EQUESTRIA, WE SHOULD BE FRIENDS!
YOU NEED TO GET SERIOUS. THE YAKS ARE NOTORIOUSLY ILL TEMPERED. IT TOOK A LOT OF WORK TO GET OUR RELATIONSHIP THIS FAR. AND PLEASE DON'T CALL ME "SHINY." I DON'T NEED A NICKNAME FROM YOU.
B.B. EX
THAT'S FINE. I SEE HOW IT IS. WELL, YOU'LL JUST HAVE TO BE DEVASTATED ON YOUR OWN WHEN SOMEONE FINALLY TELLS YOU HOW RIDICULOUS YOUR TINY GLASSES ARE.
THESE ARE IGGAAKS!
EVEN MORE REASON! YOU SHOULD NEVER WEAR SOMETHING YOU CAN'T SAY WITHOUT SPITTING ALL OVER ANOTHER PONY. LET'S GO, GENTS!
B.B. EXPRESS
GOOD RIDDANCE!
I'M GOING TO HAVE TO DO ALL THE WORK! THERE'S NO WAY I CAN LET HIM TALK TO THE YAKS!

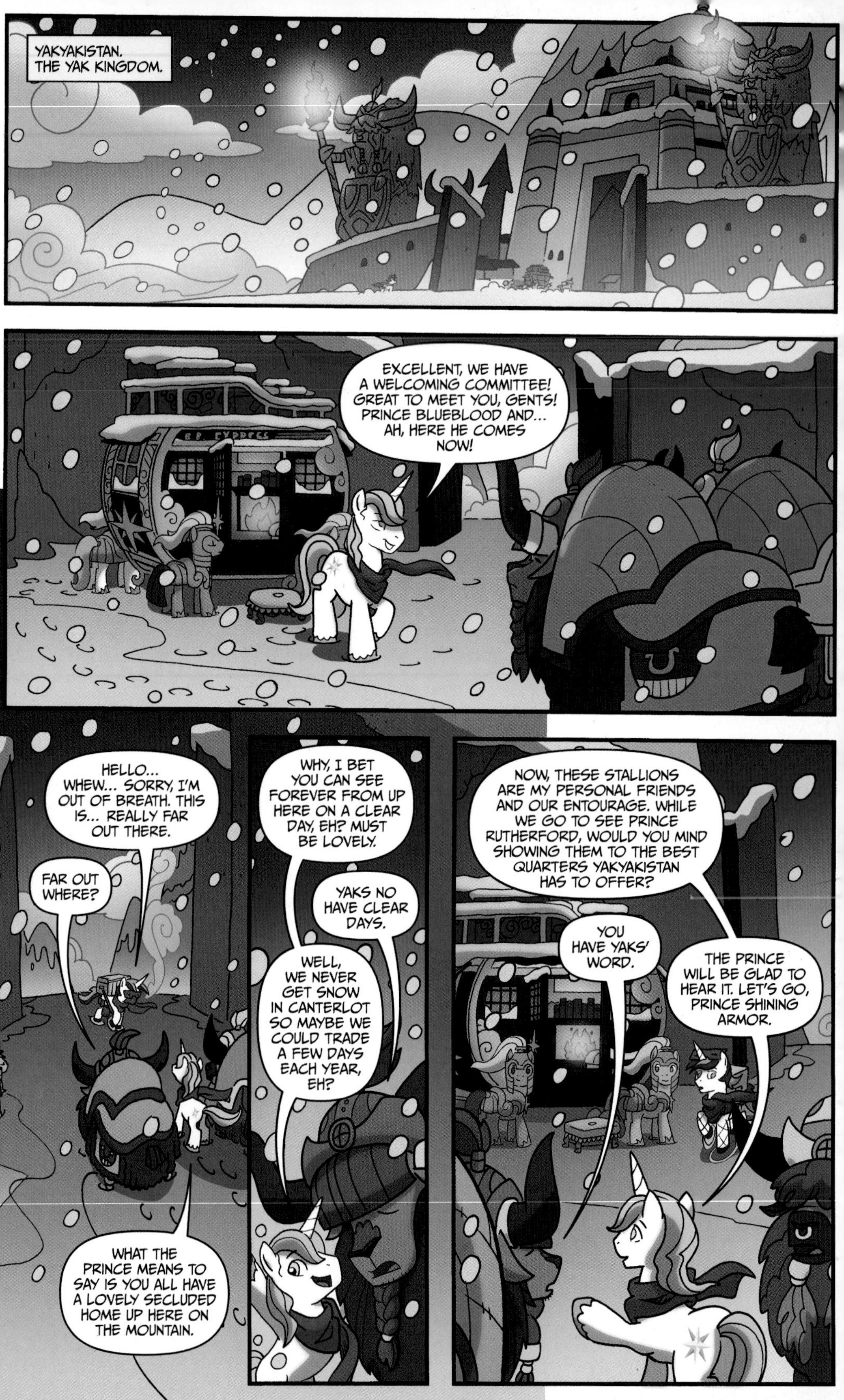
YAKYAKISTAN. THE YAK KINGDOM.
EXCELLENT, WE HAVE A WELCOMING COMMITTEE! GREAT TO MEET YOU, GENTS! PRINCE BLUEBLOOD AND... AH, HERE HE COMES NOW!
HELLO... WHEW... SORRY, I'M OUT OF BREATH. THIS IS... REALLY FAR OUT THERE.
FAR OUT WHERE?
WHAT THE PRINCE MEANS TO SAY IS YOU ALL HAVE A LOVELY SECLUDED HOME UP HERE ON THE MOUNTAIN.
WHY, I BET YOU CAN SEE FOREVER FROM UP HERE ON A CLEAR DAY, EH? MUST BE LOVELY.
YAKS NO HAVE CLEAR DAYS.
WELL, WE NEVER GET SNOW IN CANTERLOT SO MAYBE WE COULD TRADE A FEW DAYS EACH YEAR, EH?
NOW, THESE STALLIONS ARE MY PERSONAL FRIENDS AND OUR ENTOURAGE. WHILE WE GO TO SEE PRINCE RUTHERFORD, WOULD YOU MIND SHOWING THEM TO THE BEST QUARTERS YAKYAKISTAN HAS TO OFFER?
YOU HAVE YAKS' WORD.
THE PRINCE WILL BE GLAD TO HEAR IT. LET'S GO, PRINCE SHINING ARMOR.

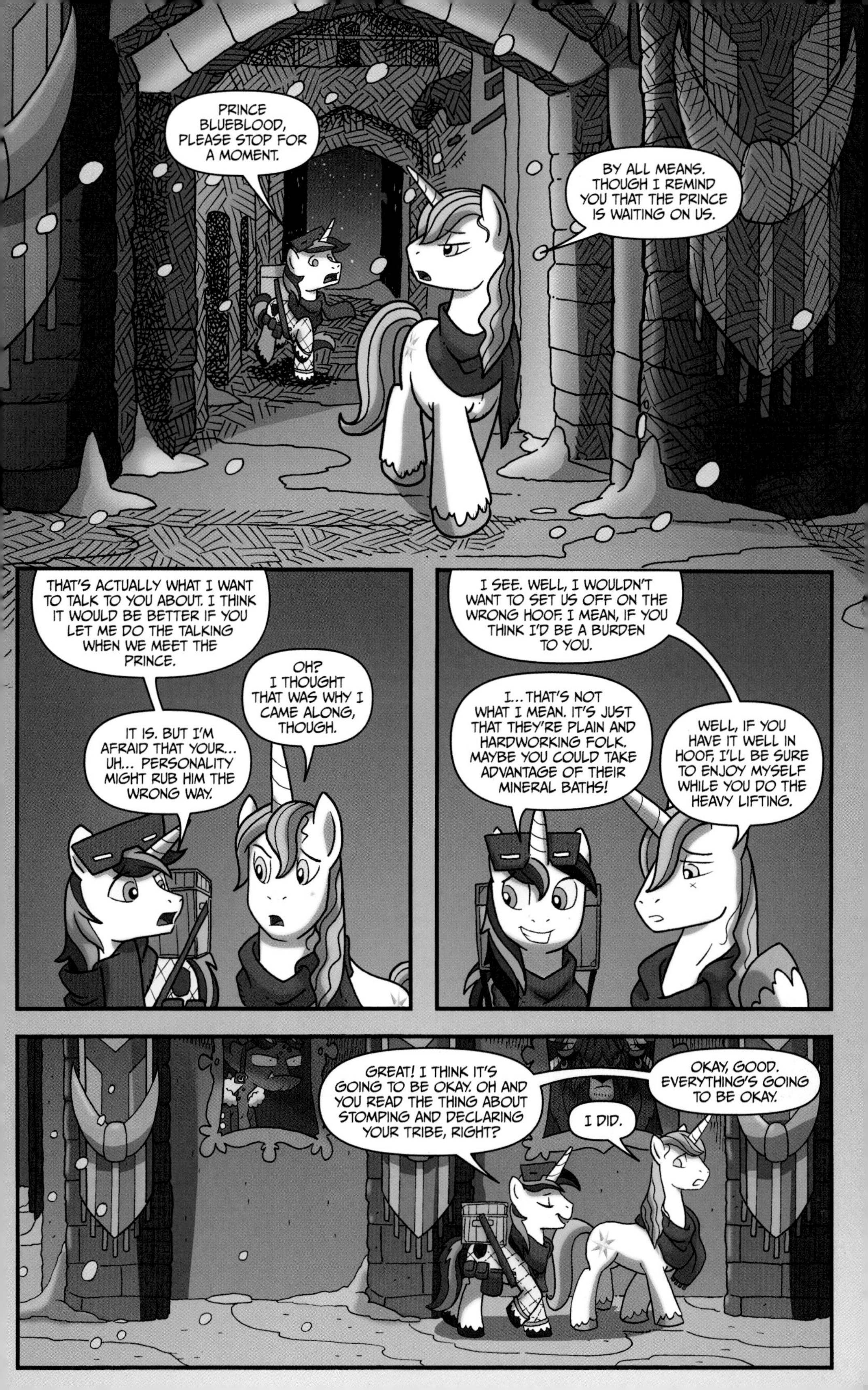
PRINCE BLUEBLOOD, PLEASE STOP FOR A MOMENT.
BY ALL MEANS. THOUGH I REMIND YOU THAT THE PRINCE IS WAITING ON US.
THAT'S ACTUALLY WHAT I WANT TO TALK TO YOU ABOUT. I THINK IT WOULD BE BETTER IF YOU LET ME DO THE TALKING WHEN WE MEET THE PRINCE.
OH? I THOUGHT THAT WAS WHY I CAME ALONG, THOUGH.
IT IS. BUT I'M AFRAID THAT YOUR... UH... PERSONALITY MIGHT RUB HIM THE WRONG WAY.
I SEE. WELL, I WOULDN'T WANT TO SET US OFF ON THE WRONG HOOF. I MEAN, IF YOU THINK I'D BE A BURDEN TO YOU.
I... THAT'S NOT WHAT I MEAN. IT'S JUST THAT THEY'RE PLAIN AND HARDWORKING FOLK. MAYBE YOU COULD TAKE ADVANTAGE OF THEIR MINERAL BATHS!
WELL, IF YOU HAVE IT WELL IN HOOF, I'LL BE SURE TO ENJOY MYSELF WHILE YOU DO THE HEAVY LIFTING.
GREAT! I THINK IT'S GOING TO BE OKAY. OH AND YOU READ THE THING ABOUT STOMPING AND DECLARING YOUR TRIBE, RIGHT?
I DID.
OKAY, GOOD. EVERYTHING'S GOING TO BE OKAY.

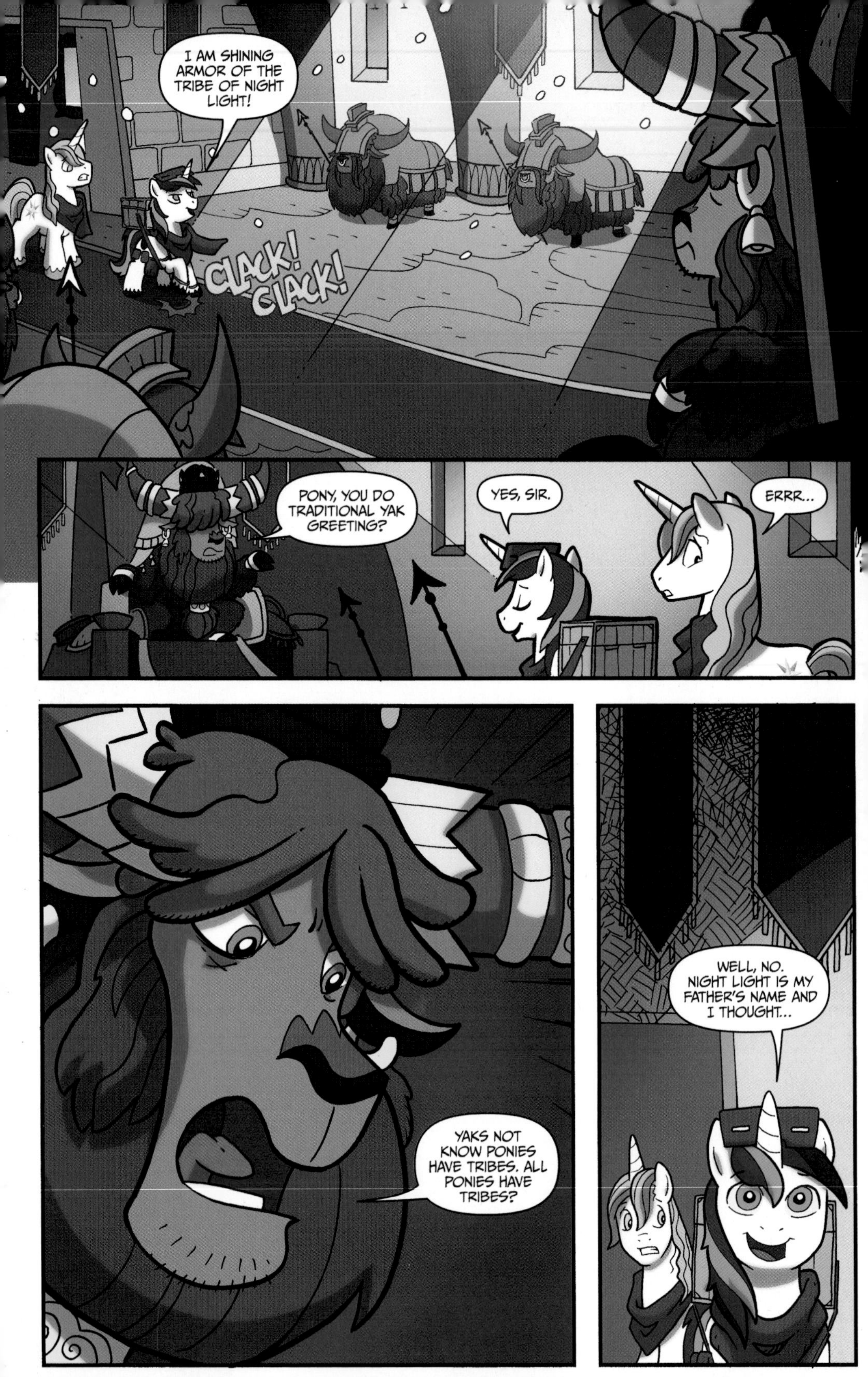
I AM SHINING ARMOR OF THE TRIBE OF NIGHT LIGHT!
CLACK! CLACK!
PONY, YOU DO TRADITIONAL YAK GREETING?
YES, SIR.
ERRR...
YAKS NOT KNOW PONIES HAVE TRIBES. ALL PONIES HAVE TRIBES?
WELL, NO. NIGHT LIGHT IS MY FATHER'S NAME AND I THOUGHT...

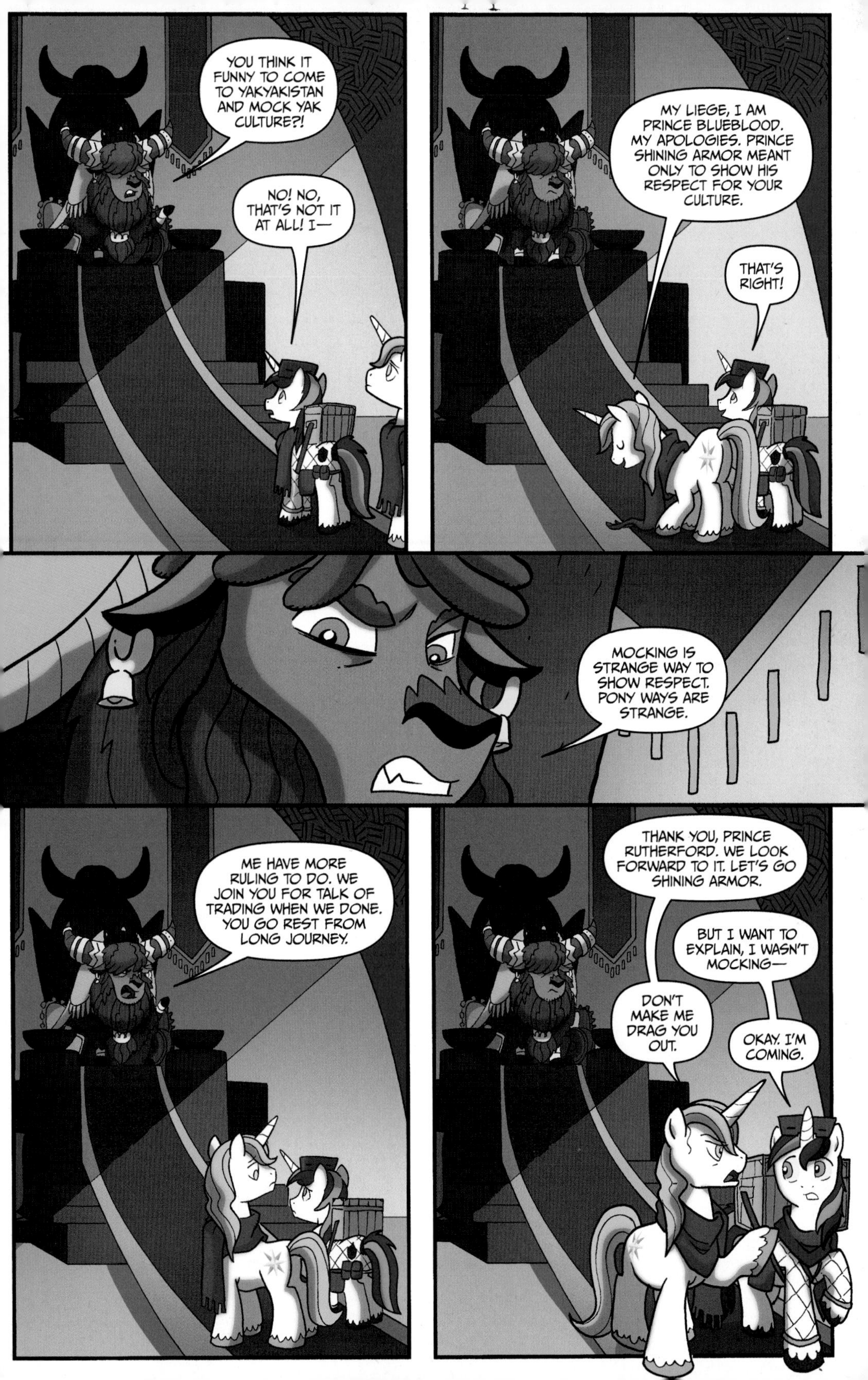
YOU THINK IT FUNNY TO COME TO YAKYAKISTAN AND MOCK YAK CULTURE?!
NO! NO, THAT'S NOT IT AT ALL! I—
MY LIEGE, I AM PRINCE BLUEBLOOD. MY APOLOGIES. PRINCE SHINING ARMOR MEANT ONLY TO SHOW HIS RESPECT FOR YOUR CULTURE.
THAT'S RIGHT!
MOCKING IS STRANGE WAY TO SHOW RESPECT. PONY WAYS ARE STRANGE.
ME HAVE MORE RULING TO DO. WE JOIN YOU FOR TALK OF TRADING WHEN WE DONE. YOU GO REST FROM LONG JOURNEY.
THANK YOU, PRINCE RUTHERFORD. WE LOOK FORWARD TO IT. LET'S GO SHINING ARMOR.
BUT I WANT TO EXPLAIN, I WASN'T MOCKING—
DON'T MAKE ME DRAG YOU OUT.
OKAY. I'M COMING.

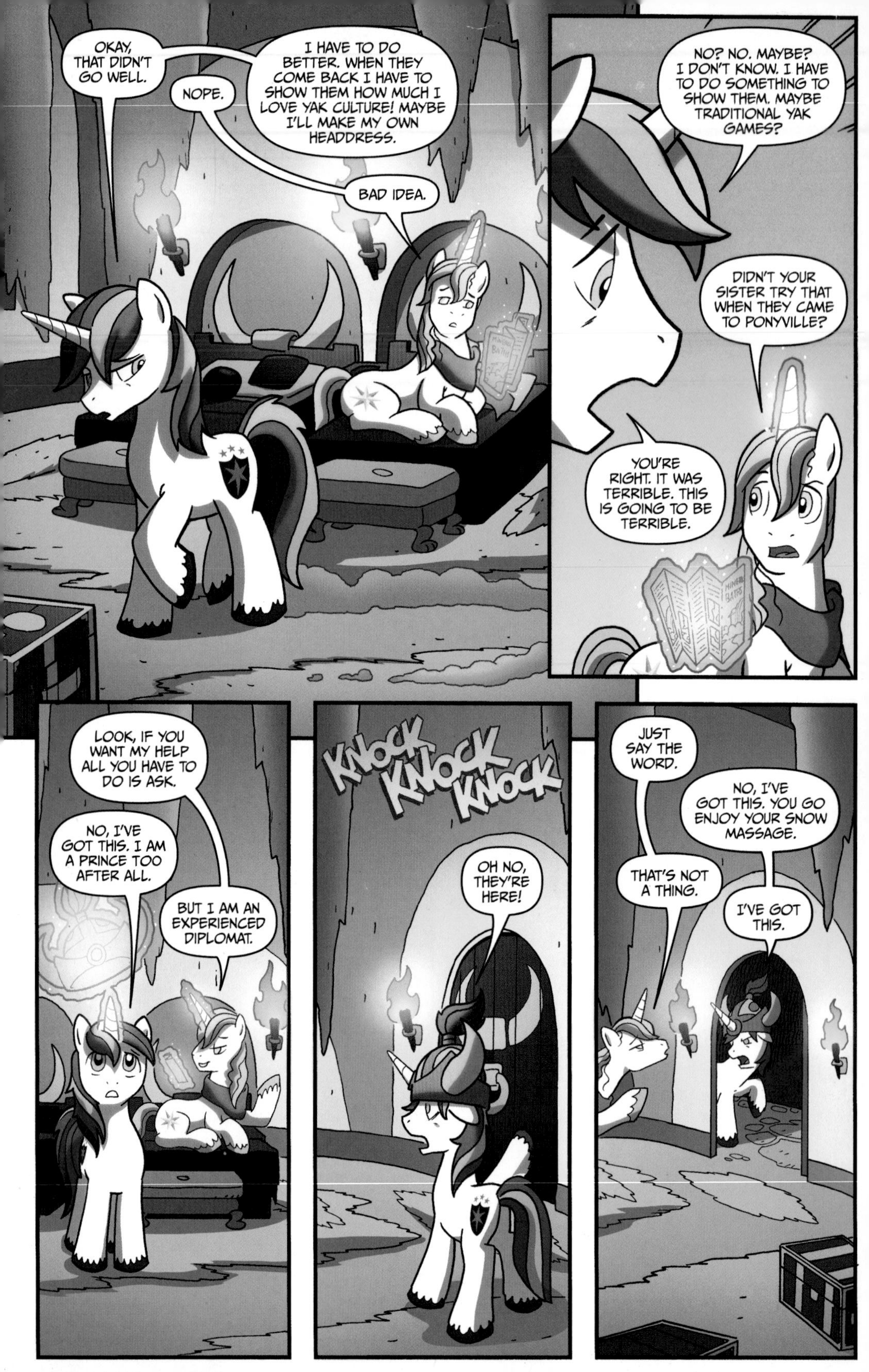
OKAY, THAT DIDN'T GO WELL.
NOPE.
I HAVE TO DO BETTER. WHEN THEY COME BACK I HAVE TO SHOW THEM HOW MUCH I LOVE YAK CULTURE! MAYBE I'LL MAKE MY OWN HEADDRESS.
BAD IDEA.
NO? NO. MAYBE? I DON'T KNOW. I HAVE TO DO SOMETHING TO SHOW THEM. MAYBE TRADITIONAL YAK GAMES?
DIDN'T YOUR SISTER TRY THAT WHEN THEY CAME TO PONYVILLE?
YOU'RE RIGHT. IT WAS TERRIBLE. THIS IS GOING TO BE TERRIBLE.
LOOK, IF YOU WANT MY HELP ALL YOU HAVE TO DO IS ASK.
NO, I'VE GOT THIS. I AM A PRINCE TOO AFTER ALL.
BUT I AM AN EXPERIENCED DIPLOMAT.
KNOCK KNOCK KNOCK
OH NO, THEY'RE HERE!
JUST SAY THE WORD.
NO, I'VE GOT THIS. YOU GO ENJOY YOUR SNOW MASSAGE.
THAT'S NOT A THING.
I'VE GOT THIS.

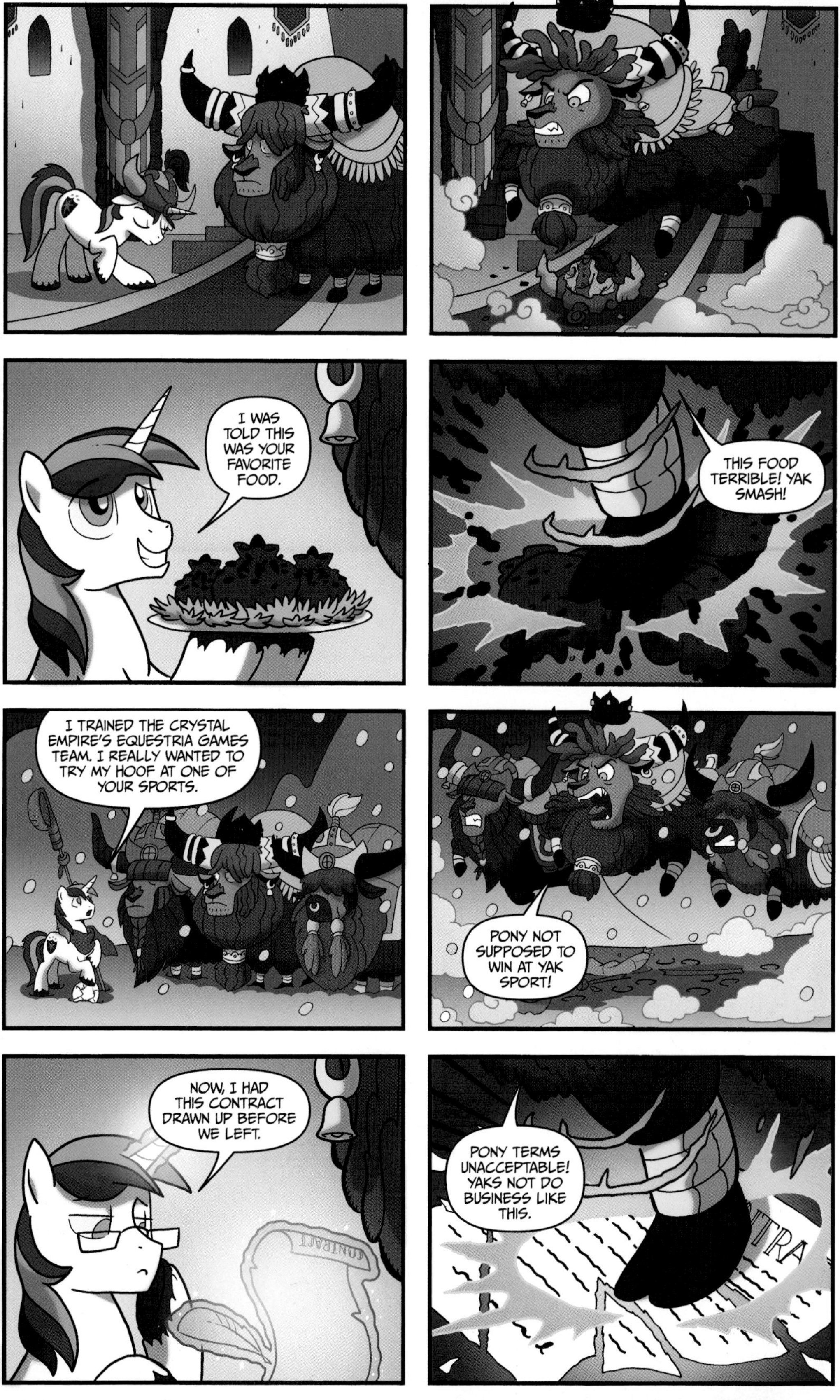
I WAS TOLD THIS WAS YOUR FAVORITE FOOD.
THIS FOOD TERRIBLE! YAK SMASH!
I TRAINED THE CRYSTAL EMPIRE'S EQUESTRIA GAMES TEAM. I REALLY WANTED TO TRY MY HOOF AT ONE OF YOUR SPORTS.
PONY NOT SUPPOSED TO WIN AT YAK SPORT!
NOW, I HAD THIS CONTRACT DRAWN UP BEFORE WE LEFT.
PONY TERMS UNACCEPTABLE! YAKS NOT DO BUSINESS LIKE THIS.

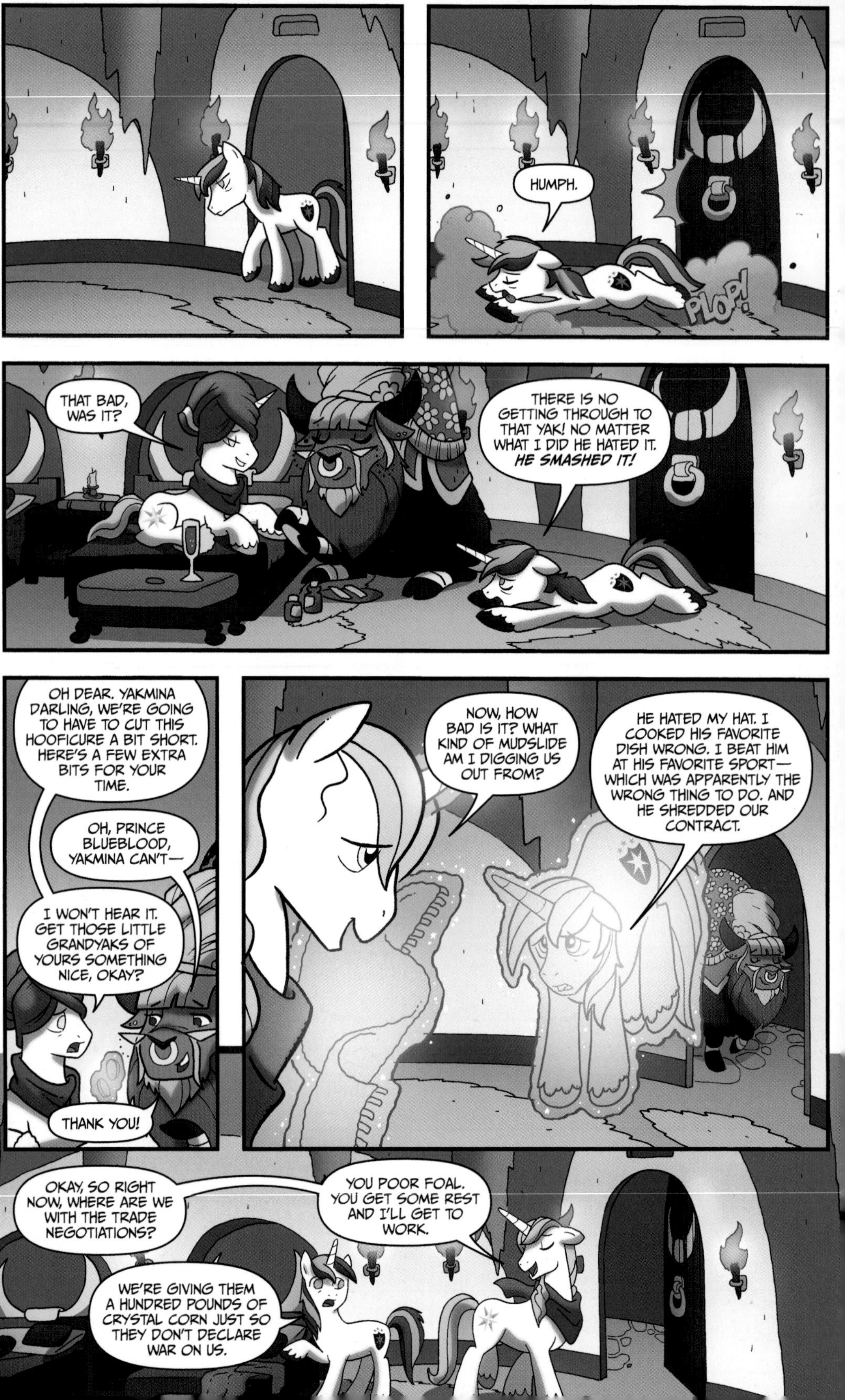
HUMPH.
PLOP!
THAT BAD, WAS IT?
THERE IS NO GETTING THROUGH TO THAT YAK! NO MATTER WHAT I DID HE HATED IT. ***HE SMASHED IT!***
OH DEAR. YAKMINA DARLING, WE'RE GOING TO HAVE TO CUT THIS HOOFICURE A BIT SHORT. HERE'S A FEW EXTRA BITS FOR YOUR TIME.
OH, PRINCE BLUEBLOOD, YAKMINA CAN'T—
I WON'T HEAR IT. GET THOSE LITTLE GRANDYAKS OF YOURS SOMETHING NICE, OKAY?
THANK YOU!
NOW, HOW BAD IS IT? WHAT KIND OF MUDSLIDE AM I DIGGING US OUT FROM?
HE HATED MY HAT. I COOKED HIS FAVORITE DISH WRONG. I BEAT HIM AT HIS FAVORITE SPORT—WHICH WAS APPARENTLY THE WRONG THING TO DO. AND HE SHREDDED OUR CONTRACT.
OKAY, SO RIGHT NOW, WHERE ARE WE WITH THE TRADE NEGOTIATIONS?
WE'RE GIVING THEM A HUNDRED POUNDS OF CRYSTAL CORN JUST SO THEY DON'T DECLARE WAR ON US.
YOU POOR FOAL. YOU GET SOME REST AND I'LL GET TO WORK.

PRINCE BLUEBLOOD'S GUIDE TO DIPLOMACY

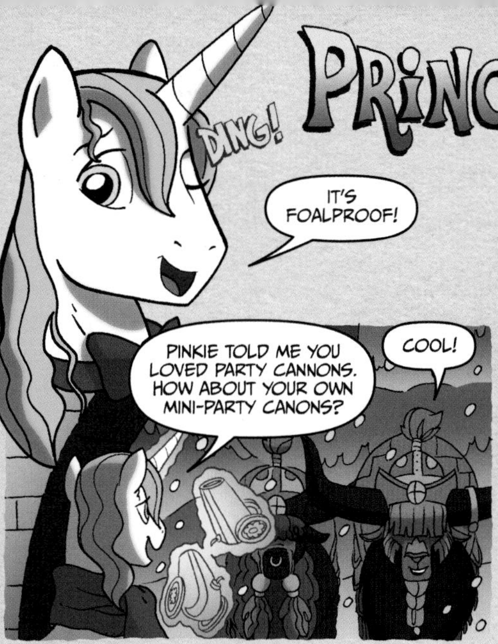
DING!
IT'S FOALPROOF!
PINKIE TOLD ME YOU LOVED PARTY CANNONS. HOW ABOUT YOUR OWN MINI-PARTY CANONS?
COOL!

Get to know their friends.

Winning over a diplomat's friends means they're hearing good things about you when you're not around.

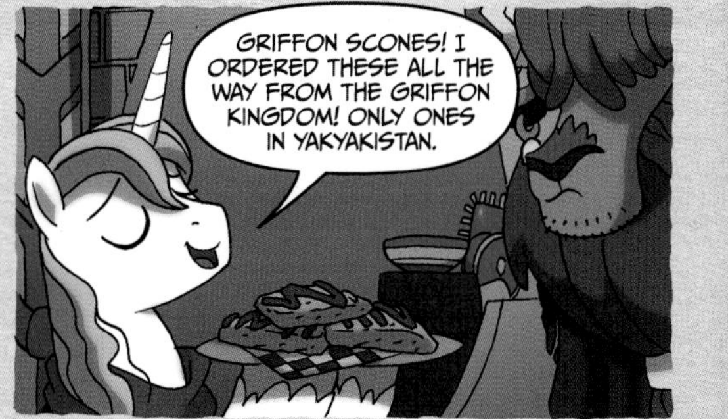
GRIFFON SCONES! I ORDERED THESE ALL THE WAY FROM THE GRIFFON KINGDOM! ONLY ONES IN YAKYAKISTAN.

Bring food.

But don't bring their food and don't claim it's the best. Make it something they'll be curious about.

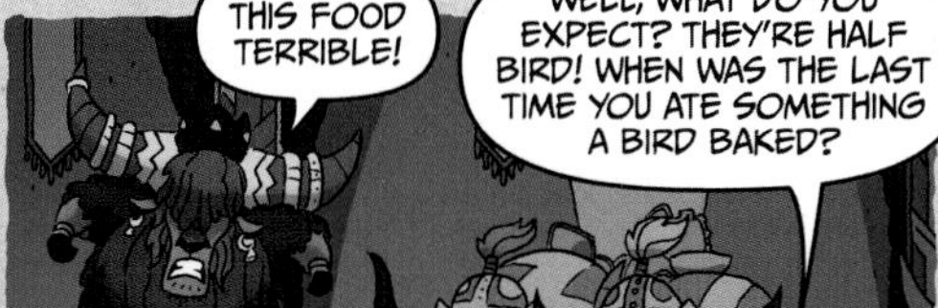
THIS FOOD TERRIBLE!
WELL, WHAT DO YOU EXPECT? THEY'RE HALF BIRD! WHEN WAS THE LAST TIME YOU ATE SOMETHING A BIRD BAKED?
HA HA HA HA!

That way if they hate them, nobody has to be insulted. You can bond over how terrible they are.

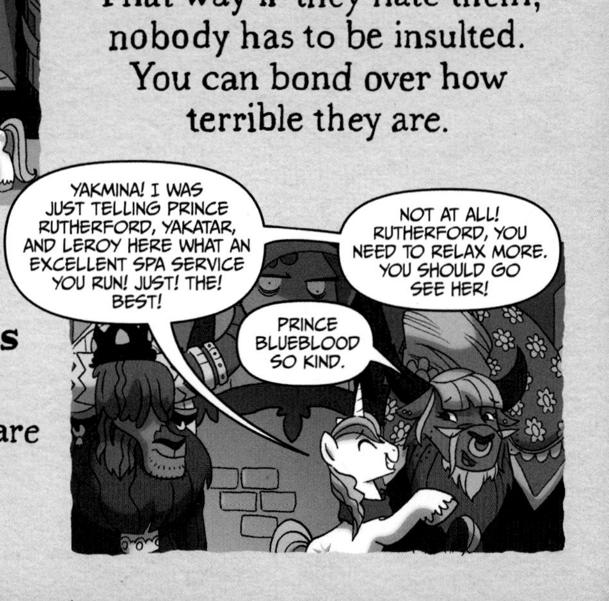
YAKMINA! I WAS JUST TELLING PRINCE RUTHERFORD, YAKATAR, AND LEROY HERE WHAT AN EXCELLENT SPA SERVICE YOU RUN! JUST! THE! BEST!
NOT AT ALL! RUTHERFORD, YOU NEED TO RELAX MORE. YOU SHOULD GO SEE HER!
PRINCE BLUEBLOOD SO KIND.

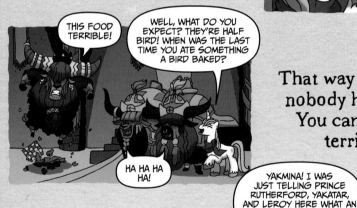

Remember everypony's name all the time.

It shows ponies that you care (even if you don't.)

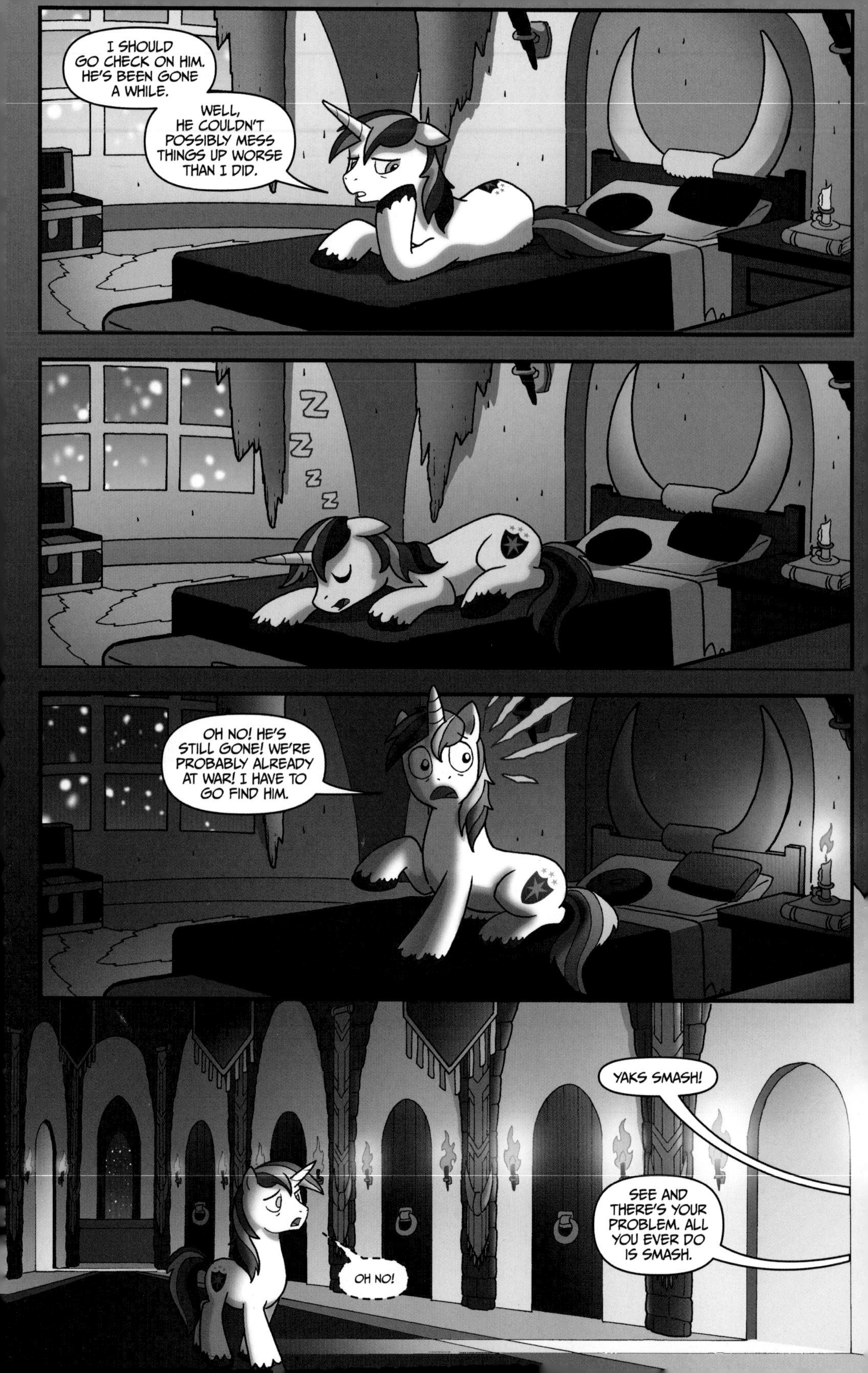
I SHOULD GO CHECK ON HIM. HE'S BEEN GONE A WHILE.
WELL, HE COULDN'T POSSIBLY MESS THINGS UP WORSE THAN I DID.
Z Z Z Z
OH NO! HE'S STILL GONE! WE'RE PROBABLY ALREADY AT WAR! I HAVE TO GO FIND HIM.
YAKS SMASH!
SEE AND THERE'S YOUR PROBLEM. ALL YOU EVER DO IS SMASH.
OH NO!

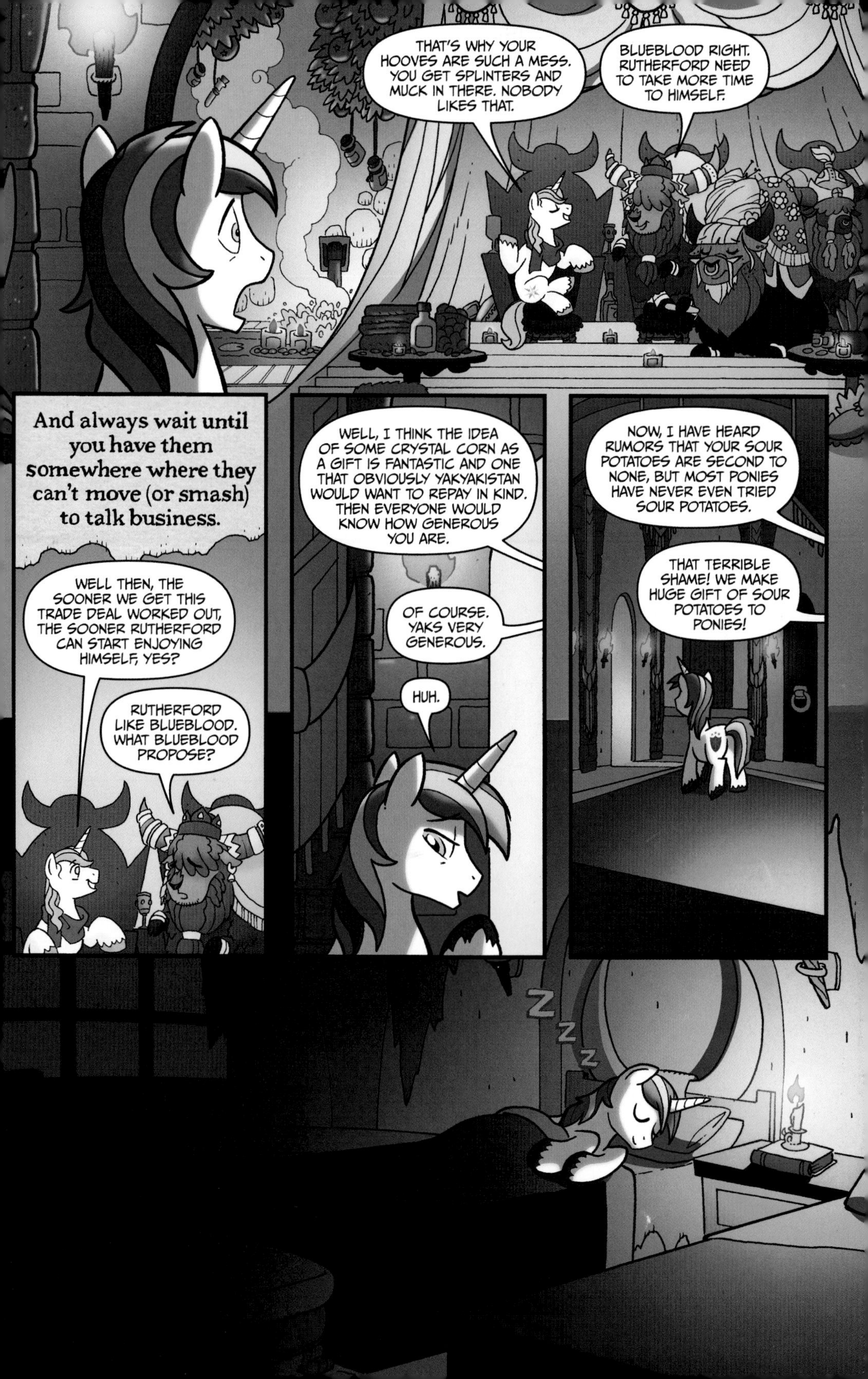
THAT'S WHY YOUR HOOVES ARE SUCH A MESS. YOU GET SPLINTERS AND MUCK IN THERE. NOBODY LIKES THAT.
BLUEBLOOD RIGHT. RUTHERFORD NEED TO TAKE MORE TIME TO HIMSELF.
And always wait until you have them somewhere where they can't move (or smash) to talk business.
WELL THEN, THE SOONER WE GET THIS TRADE DEAL WORKED OUT, THE SOONER RUTHERFORD CAN START ENJOYING HIMSELF, YES?
RUTHERFORD LIKE BLUEBLOOD. WHAT BLUEBLOOD PROPOSE?
WELL, I THINK THE IDEA OF SOME CRYSTAL CORN AS A GIFT IS FANTASTIC AND ONE THAT OBVIOUSLY YAKYAKISTAN WOULD WANT TO REPAY IN KIND. THEN EVERYONE WOULD KNOW HOW GENEROUS YOU ARE.
OF COURSE. YAKS VERY GENEROUS.
HUH.
NOW, I HAVE HEARD RUMORS THAT YOUR SOUR POTATOES ARE SECOND TO NONE, BUT MOST PONIES HAVE NEVER EVEN TRIED SOUR POTATOES.
THAT TERRIBLE SHAME! WE MAKE HUGE GIFT OF SOUR POTATOES TO PONIES!
Z Z Z

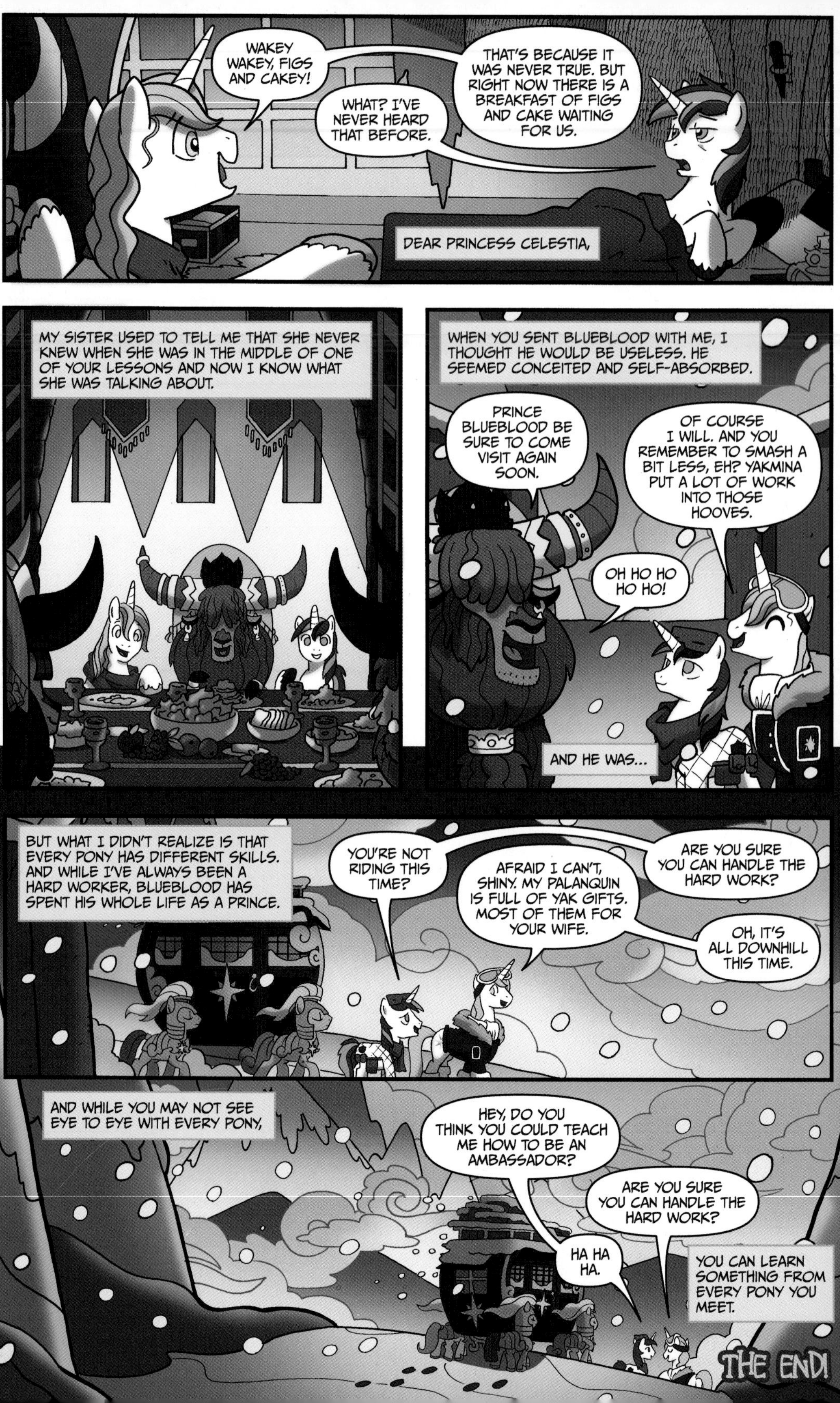
WAKEY WAKEY, FIGS AND CAKEY!
WHAT? I'VE NEVER HEARD THAT BEFORE.
THAT'S BECAUSE IT WAS NEVER TRUE. BUT RIGHT NOW THERE IS A BREAKFAST OF FIGS AND CAKE WAITING FOR US.
DEAR PRINCESS CELESTIA,
MY SISTER USED TO TELL ME THAT SHE NEVER KNEW WHEN SHE WAS IN THE MIDDLE OF ONE OF YOUR LESSONS AND NOW I KNOW WHAT SHE WAS TALKING ABOUT.
WHEN YOU SENT BLUEBLOOD WITH ME, I THOUGHT HE WOULD BE USELESS. HE SEEMED CONCEITED AND SELF-ABSORBED.
PRINCE BLUEBLOOD BE SURE TO COME VISIT AGAIN SOON.
OF COURSE I WILL. AND YOU REMEMBER TO SMASH A BIT LESS, EH? YAKMINA PUT A LOT OF WORK INTO THOSE HOOVES.
OH HO HO HO HO!
AND HE WAS...
BUT WHAT I DIDN'T REALIZE IS THAT EVERY PONY HAS DIFFERENT SKILLS. AND WHILE I'VE ALWAYS BEEN A HARD WORKER, BLUEBLOOD HAS SPENT HIS WHOLE LIFE AS A PRINCE.
YOU'RE NOT RIDING THIS TIME?
AFRAID I CAN'T, SHINY. MY PALANQUIN IS FULL OF YAK GIFTS. MOST OF THEM FOR YOUR WIFE.
ARE YOU SURE YOU CAN HANDLE THE HARD WORK?
OH, IT'S ALL DOWNHILL THIS TIME.
AND WHILE YOU MAY NOT SEE EYE TO EYE WITH EVERY PONY,
HEY, DO YOU THINK YOU COULD TEACH ME HOW TO BE AN AMBASSADOR?
ARE YOU SURE YOU CAN HANDLE THE HARD WORK?
HA HA HA.
YOU CAN LEARN SOMETHING FROM EVERY PONY YOU MEET.
THE END!

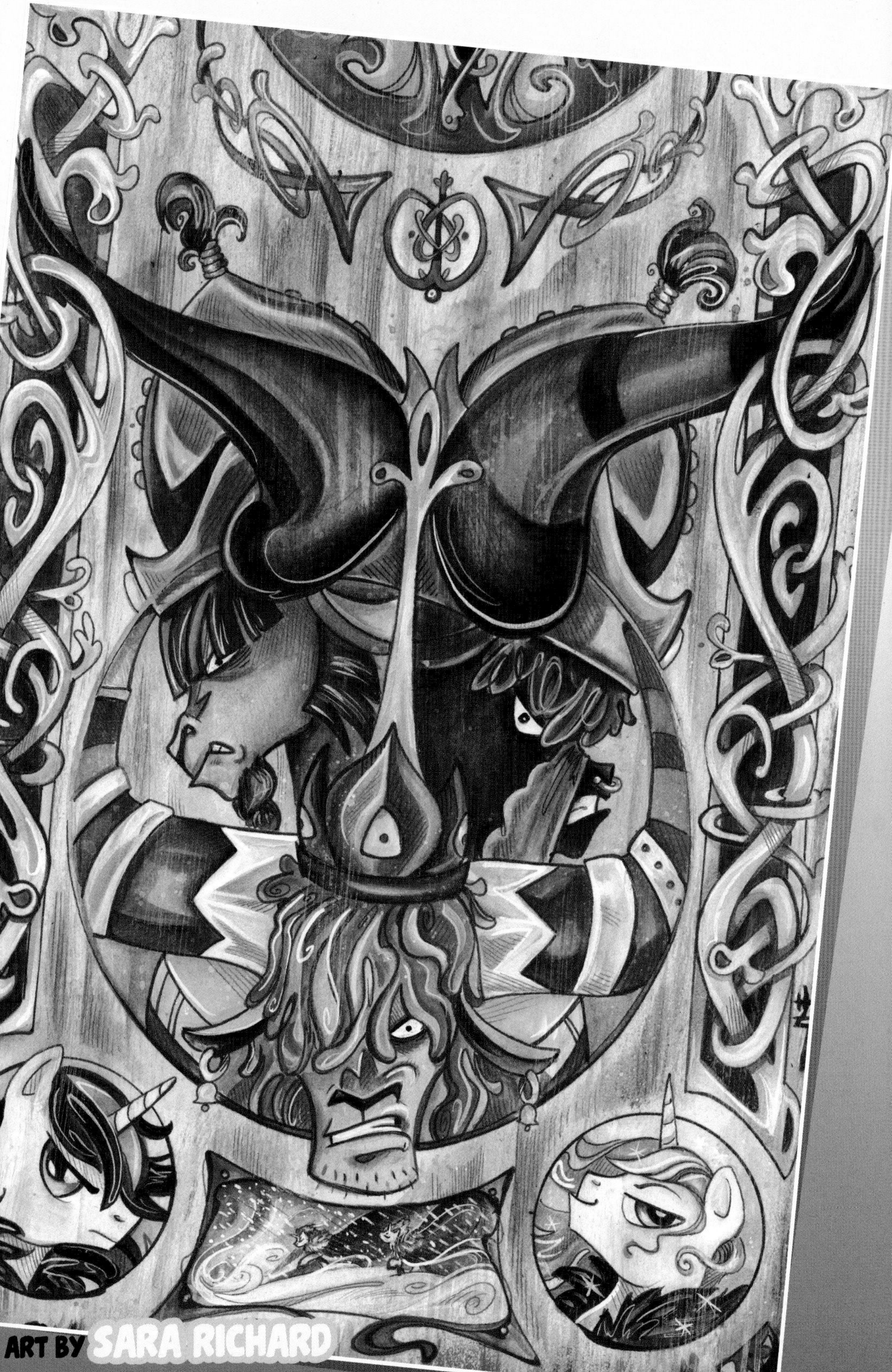

ART BY SARA RICHARD

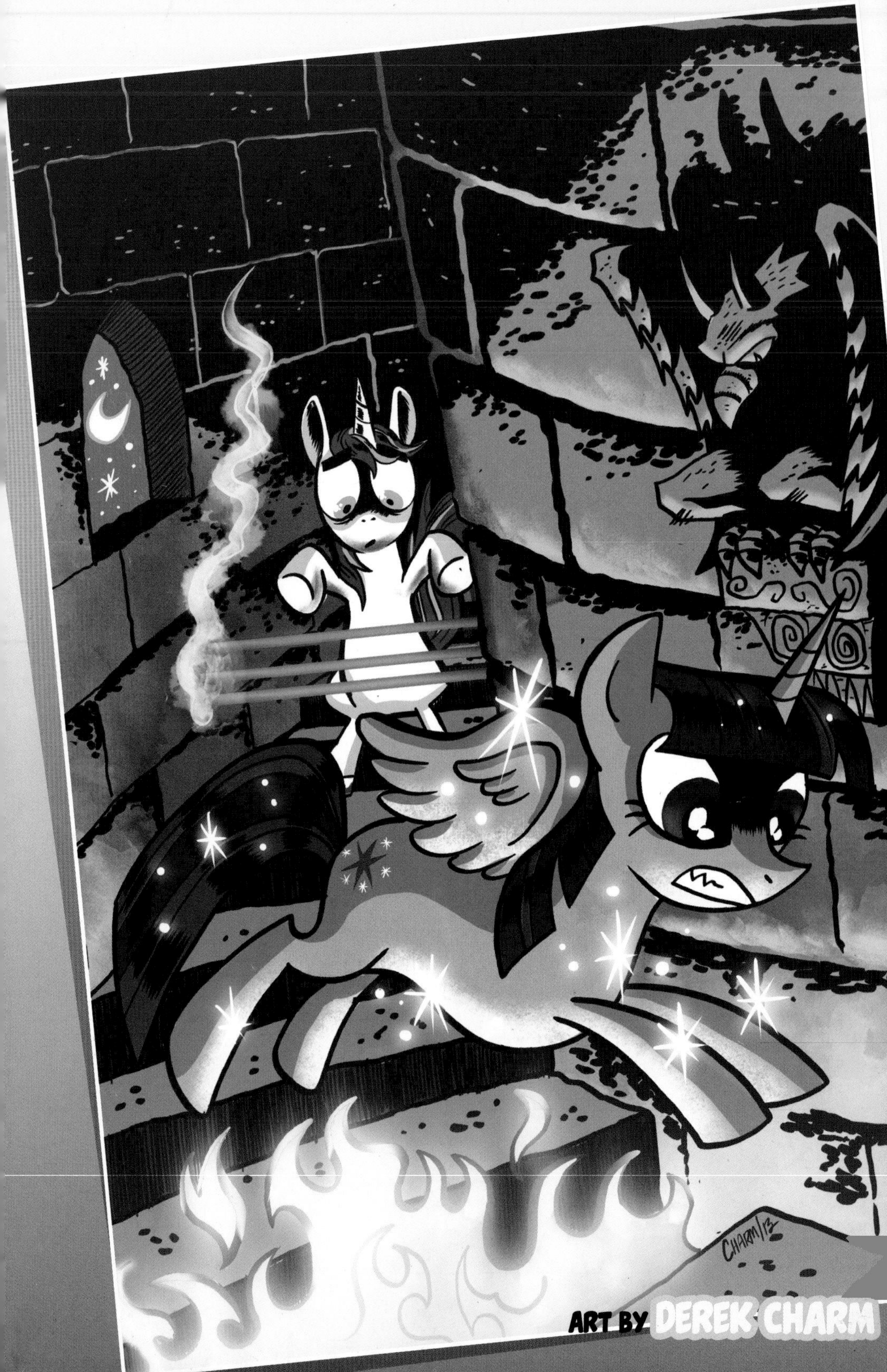
CHARM/13
ART BY DEREK CHARM

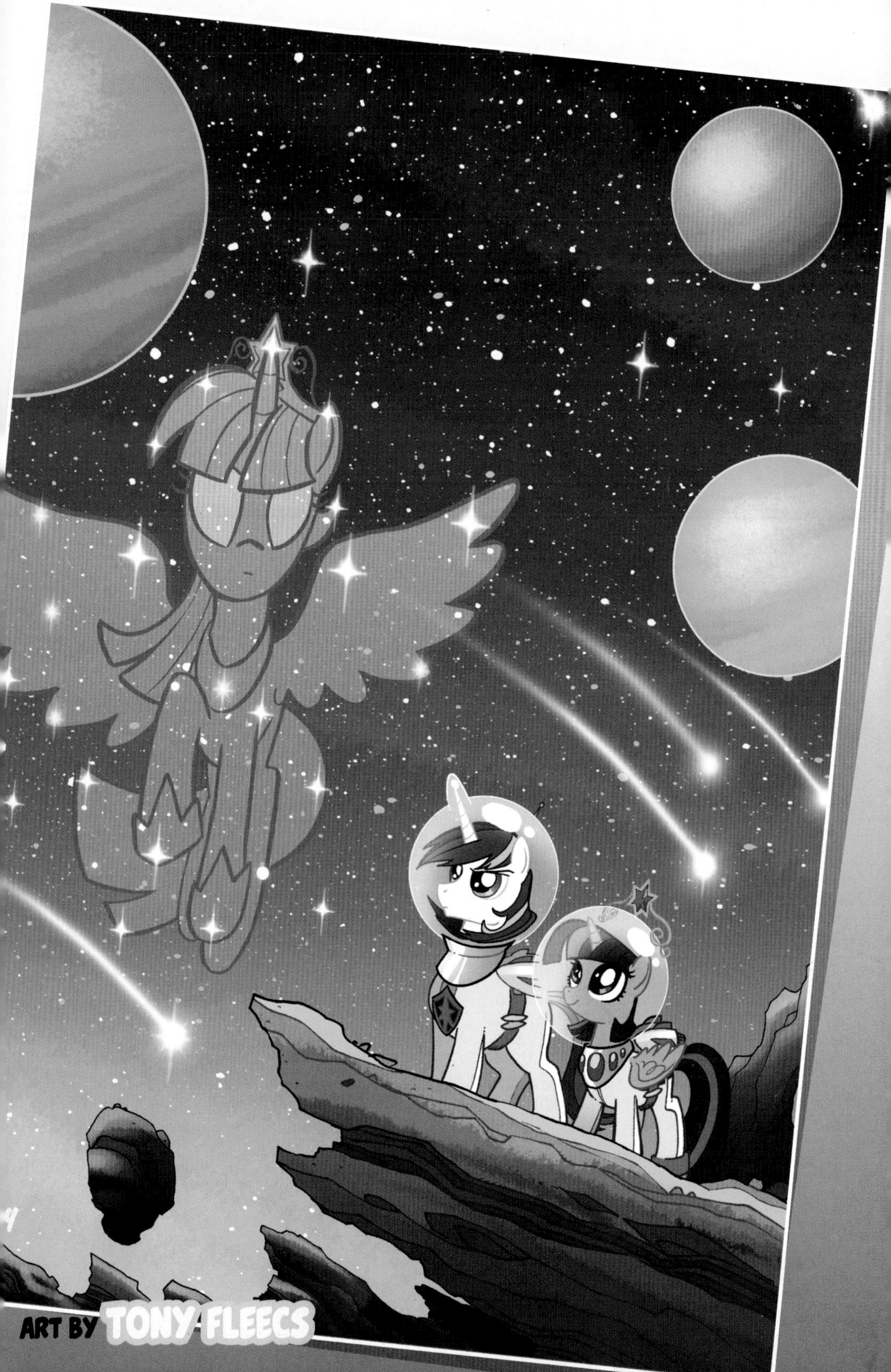

ART BY TONY FLEECS